30

THE LEFT-HAND PATH

Day Hanly laid a shovel across his daddy's head and then quit the farm with John Tillet. But it wasn't long before they parted company. The path that Tillet chose led him to an embattled group of German farmers, trying to forge a community despite their hostile native Texan neighbours. Day takes the left-hand path which could lead only to damnation. However, when their paths cross again, Tillet, the man of the law, will come up against Day, the outlaw . . .

Books by Jack Gallagher
in the Linford Western Library:

SON OF LIGHTNING

JACK GALLAGHER

THE LEFT-HAND PATH

Complete and Unabridged

LINFORD
Leicester

First published in Great Britain in 1997 by
Robert Hale Limited
London

First Linford Edition
published 1998
by arrangement with
Robert Hale Limited
London

British Library CIP Data

Gallagher, Jack, *1953* –
    The left-hand path.—Large print ed.—
Linford western library
1. Western stories
2. Large type books
I. Title
823.9′14 [F]

ISBN 0–7089–5327–1

Published by
F. A. Thorpe (Publishing) Ltd.
Anstey, Leicestershire

Set by Words & Graphics Ltd.
Anstey, Leicestershire
Printed and bound in Great Britain by
T. J. International Ltd., Padstow, Cornwall

This book is printed on acid-free paper

1

'Mule, put down that sack and grab this shovel. You look just like a mule with your two little stupid eyes, you know that? I guess I've found a name for you.'

Tillet managed to fend off the shovel with his left hand as it flew towards him. He dumped the hundredweight sack of corn on the cart and straightened his aching back.

'Mule, don't tarry. Pa said, 'Get cousin John to muck out the hogs after he's loaded the corn for the mill'. And you know what a mean son-of-a-bitch Pa is, so you better shift.'

Tillet knew. Since his mother had died and he had come to live with her brother Timothy, he'd discovered that meanness and Bible-thumping ran in the Hanly family. And while cousin Day showed no sign of being very

1

keen on religion, the meanness was all there.

'I reckon your pa's got two shovels.'

Day screwed up his eyes and put on a bumpkin's voice. 'Ah reckon . . . oh Lord, you sure are back-country, Mule. Don't worry, I'm gonna give you a hand. Come on.'

Day sprang up on the fence and balanced with one foot on the top cross-rail and one on the next down. 'Jump over there.' He pointed to the stretch of fence along from him. 'The gate's knotted up tighter'n hell.'

Tillet picked up the shovel. As usual, he felt awkward and stupid-looking under cousin Day's mocking eyes. He put his foot on the rail and tried to jump up as easily as Day to show that he could do it. There was a dry crack as his weight came down on the top rail. His feet hit the ground first but his weight was thrown forward. He managed a couple of running steps trying to find his balance before his feet skidded off in different directions on the muck of the hog-pen floor and he felt the wind slammed out of his lungs.

Day was sitting on the top rail of the fence beating his thighs with his fists. 'That damn' timber was rotted drier than a biscuit.'

When Tillet raised up his head and glared at him, Day laughed harder. 'Oh Lord, you look just like Pa when you give me that mean look. Hanly blood must run strong in you all right. Thank God I've got Ma's blood in me.'

Tillet stood up, black from knees to chest. Day took a second to have a good look and began to laugh in earnest. Tillet felt the blood come into his face. He hated to be laughed at more than anything in the world.

His mother, with her man's coat and work-boots, had worn her poverty with a stubborn pride. And she'd made him wear it too. She always had her donation for the church collection-plate, but there wasn't another child in the country schoolhouse, ill-clad as many of them were, who couldn't afford to laugh at Tillet's rags. And one day, out in front of the class, as he bent for a log to feed the schoolhouse stove, the threadbare seat of his pants had come apart. As they'd laughed, he'd caught a funny look from the schoolmaster and realized to his burning shame that his eyes were wet. He felt like crying now. Eighteen years old or not.

'Say, you are a sorry sight. I think we'll take you down in the rye and stand you in the middle of the field as a scarecrow.'

Rage swelled inside him and without seeming to make any choice in the matter he found himself going for Day.

Day and the fence both went over. He kept going through Day's fists, taking the punches without feeling them, went into him bent double, hooking his arms around him, carrying them both at a run through the cabbage patch, levelling the ridges, mashing the heads into the mud, through the peppers and the onions, until they crashed into the slats of the hen-coop. A flurry of squawking hens flew out of the opening as the coop slid off its bearing timbers and splintered under the weight of both of them landing on it. Even in the heat of battle Tillet felt a foreboding. He could see his Uncle Timothy's bristly eyebrows twitching with anger as they took in the wreckage.

Day scrambled to his feet and his eyes glittered with excitement between his raised fists. Tillet was stronger than Day and knew that if he could come properly to grips with him he could bring him down. Day's fists smacked into his face but he kept going doggedly forward, and then at last he got a grip and they were stumbling over the downed fence into the hog-pen, staggering this way and that while the pigs squealed and tried to escape them.

Tillet got his arm round Day's neck

and slowly dragged his head down. Day was bent double and Tillet was summoning the strength for a final effort to bring him to the ground when he felt a leg tangled in his and then he was on his back with Day on top of him, but with his neck still locked in Tillet's arms.

Day slapped his shoulder with an open palm and wheezed, 'OK, you're down. Leave go my head and I'll let you up.'

Tillet could only see Day's forehead, but it was red as a tomato. 'I don't reckon I'm down. I reckon we're both down.'

'I'm on top, so you're down.'

'I don't reckon so. I got hold of your head and I could punch you senseless if I want.'

They did not hear the horse approach, and when the voice spoke it was right above them.

'Get on your feet the both of you.'

At the sound of the slow, flat, Scots-Irish burr, Tillet let go of Day's neck and, coated with muck from head to feet, they slowly picked themselves up under the black gaze of Timothy Hanly.

Hanly was ponderous of speech and movement. His long upper body bent forward in the saddle, he took his time to look round and let his eyes take in the uprooted fence, the smashed coop, and the mangled plants. His spiky eyebrows twitched absently every now and then. He turned back to face them. His lower lip hung open slackly. His sullen black eyes looked Day up and down.

'I wonder why you put me in mind of your mother standing there? Maybe it's the mire and muck all over you . . . Mind, she wore her filth on the inside. Outside, she was presentable enough . . . Aye, presentable enough, I suppose you'd say. I'm thinking, on the day of judgement she won't have her finery and her frippery or her perfumes and powders to disguise her. Aye . . . then the stench of her harlot's soul will turn the stomach of the Lord God Himself.'

He lowered himself wearily to the ground and stood gazing at the ruined plants, the big muscles of his stooped shoulders dragging his jacket tight.

'I gave you a man's trust, but you chose to play the child.' He looked at Day and shook his head. 'Ach, there isn't the makings of a man in you. Well, if you behave like a child, like a child you'll be chastised.' He turned and began to walk towards the house. 'Come in and take your punishment.'

Day, his shoulders hunched and his head down, glared darkly at his father's back. 'You ain't using that cane on me.'

Day's father stopped and slowly turned. Day shuffled uneasily under his gaze. Tillet felt like a schoolboy back in the classroom. 'You'll come inside and take your punishment.' His heavy gaze settled on Tillet. 'You, boy — you'll take yours too if you want to bide under my roof.' He continued

8

walking towards the house without looking back. 'If I have to come out, it'll be with the bullwhip.'

The whites of Day's eyes gleamed in his face still flushed from the fight. He shuffled a couple of steps forward and Tillet began to move as well. He did not want to be beaten like a child by Day's father. Not by any man. The road lay just across the field. But if he left his Uncle Timothy there wasn't a soul in the world he could turn to.

Day stumbled back over the downed fence and lifted the shovel out of the muck of the pen. Tillet watched with his heart pounding in his chest, as Day hurried after his father, raising the shovel as he ran. Uncle Timothy's bald head with its circle of wiry grey hair did not turn. The shovel landed with a dull clang on the bare patch of skull.

Day's father sagged down on one knee and raised a hand to his head. The shovel came down again and hit his hand. Day's father sank down on hands and knees. His head wasn't cut but his right hand was red with blood.

Tillet snapped out of his shock and ran forward. Day was standing over his father, shaking the shovel as if nerving himself for another blow. Tillet grabbed the handle and wrenched it out of his hands.

Day crouched down and snatched the pistol his father wore on his hip. He backed off a few steps and cocked the hammer

'You bastard,' he screamed at the back of his father's head. His eyes were wild, gleaming with tears.

His father awkwardly turned himself round. He fell heavily on his buttocks. His eyes were glittering with alarm. The slack of his jowls shook as he shouted, 'You'd strike your own father, would you? May the hand wither that you raised to your father. God's curse on ye.'

'Shut up, you bastard. You asked for it and asked for it and now by God I'm going to give it to you.'

'No, Day.' Tillet's mouth was dry. His voice came out hoarse. 'They'll hang you.'

Day was trembling so hard that Tillet was afraid he would jerk off a shot whether he meant to or not.

His father threw his arm across his eyes and yelled, 'You whore's son. Shoot if you're going to shoot.'

'By Christ, you ask for it one more time and I'll give it to you.' Day's voice was already hoarse and ragged.

Tillet closed on him and grabbed hold of the gun. Day let him pull his arm aside, but his grip tightened on the gun when Tillet tried to take it away from him.

'Leave go the gun.'

'No, Day . . .'

'Leave her go. I won't shoot.'

Day's voice sounded calmer. Tillet released his grip and stepped away.

'I ain't gonna shoot him. He ain't worth it.'

His father uncovered his eyes. 'By

God, I'll not keep you after this.' He was still yelling, but Tillet could see it was mostly to disguise his fear. 'I've done my father's part. God knows I have. I've kept you and clothed you and this is my payment. The Devil's marked you for his. Go on, clear out. Like your dirty whore of a mother before you.'

Day turned and started back to where the mare stood staring fixedly at them.

'From this day I make you my son, John.' He raised his voice and shouted at Day's back. 'Let him go. No good will become of him. Stay you here, and if you work hard and lead a Christian life, I'll give you my oath on the Bible you'll inherit all.'

Day turned back. 'You want to stay with that sanctimonious son-of-a-bitch?' He gave a contemptuous jerk of the head to where his father still sat on the ground.

'What you figuring to do?'

'Hell, I don't know. But if you

want to come along we can figure it out between us. I know I've given you a hard time, but listen — if I call a man a friend, I ain't joking. There ain't no half the way with me. So it's up to you.' Day left him standing there. When he'd mounted his father's horse, he rode it back and said, 'Well?'

'I reckon I'll come along.'

'Then shake on it.' Day reached down and grasped his hand. 'Jump up, Johnny.' Tillet stuck his foot in the stirrup and Day helped haul him up behind. 'I tell you, whatever we do, I swear it won't be bustin' sod.' Day pointed his father's Colt in the air and fired a blast that made the mare rear back and almost tumble Tillet off. With a whoop he kicked its flanks and they jumped over the smashed chicken coop and began to gallop across the bean field.

'Ride,' Day's father yelled. Neither of them looked back. 'North or south, east or west.' His voice sounded small, like the cawing of a crow lost in the high stacked clouds. 'There's many a road to choose but only one journey's end. Only one journey's end for you: you're bound for Hell.'

2

They took the trail west of the Sabine, through the cypress swamps and cotton fields, intending to cross the Trinity and reach the cattle country of the Panhandle. One walked while the other took a turn in the saddle. They begged food from travellers and sometimes worked for their supper on the homesteads, but mostly they went hungry.

It was in the hope of begging something to eat that they tried to hail the black-suited figure mounted on a white horse that they spotted on the trail ahead, but either he was out of earshot or he chose to ignore them.

'I'm going to ride after him,' said Day. 'I'm that hungry if the Devil offered me a cup of coffee and a pancake for my everlasting soul, I don't believe I'd dicker.'

The rider on the white horse disappeared around a turn in the road and Day followed him out of sight, leaving Tillet to shuffle along through the dust of the trail.

He was tired and hungry, but apart from that he felt good. It was the first time in his life he'd felt free. His own man. It was true Day took the upper hand a bit, but it seemed only natural. Day was full of notions and plans. He was full of stories about highwaymen, or the old Romans, or buried treasure in the jungles south of the border. It shook his ideas up to listen to him.

Day came riding back over the rise. 'Sure is strange. You'd swear he disappeared into thin air. He would've had to put on a gallop to make the next turn of the trail before I spotted him.'

'Maybe he went into the woods.'

'Yeah, I guess.'

They caught another glimpse of the rider some miles later but lost him again. They had to put up with their hunger until, in the afternoon, they came to the bank of a wide, sluggish stream where a wagon was drawn up and a man and a girl sat beside a camp-fire. The smell of brewing coffee came to them over the clear air.

The man cocked his head warily at them. He was somewhere over fifty, solid as a bull about the shoulders and chest and with a healthy growth of white hair. The girl was plump and softly curved. Wisps of her fine blonde hair had escaped from their binding and floated in the breeze. After giving them a shy glance, she continued kneading dough on a board laid on the ground. There was a gentle patience about her movements that made Tillet feel peaceful to watch her.

'Mister, I ain't drunk nothing but plain water in three days and I'd call it Christian of you to give me a mouthful of that coffee,' Day said.

'Well, I'm a Christian, I hope.' The high Irish brogue sounded guarded and he kept his head cocked suspiciously.

Day lowered his head and put on a

pleading look. 'Just a drink of coffee, mister, and maybe a piece of that bread to stop the hunger gnawing at us . . .'

The man gave a sudden jerk of his body. 'Oh, come on lads. I see you're in the mood to eat, all right. Join the camp and welcome.'

Day slurped his coffee and swallowed with a loud sigh. 'Oh Lord, that tastes good.'

'There's nothing like a cup of coffee at the right time — unless it's a nice cup of tea. Yes, I'm sorry for looking you over a bit doubtful just there, for I see you're decent lads, but the truth is, I'm far from home — all the way from New York, in fact — and then, I find myself responsible for the welfare of two young ladies — two young ladies of such surpassing loveliness, that I'm not even sure I can trust myself with them.'

The girl blushed and ducked her head at this.

'There now,' said the man. 'And if

you can't trust me, then who can you trust?' He gave a nod of his head in the direction of the wagon and Tillet saw that a black dicky and dog-collar hung from one of the hooks on the side.

'You a reverend?' Day asked.

'Father Eugene Slattery, from St Mary Magdalene of the Bronx, New York.' The priest stuck out a big hand that looked as if it could crush your knuckles, but his shake was brief and limp.

'Day Hanly.'

'John Tillet.'

'And this angel is Anna Miller.'

'It sure is a pleasure to meet you.' Day gave a slow bow and a smile, keeping his eyes fixed on her face all the time.

'Howdy,' was all Tillet could come up with.

She replied hesitantly. There was an accent to her voice.

'You sound Dutch or maybe Swedish, miss,' said Day.

The girl glanced nervously at the

priest. Tillet was sorry that they were making her uneasy. Father Slattery said, 'Anna has recently come to America from Germany. I'm taking her to her uncle, who has a farm near the town of Lodestar. And it's to Lodestar that I have also been commissioned to bring the word of God — and Bishop Feeney. A community of German farmers have settled there, and as they're all of them good Catholics, they've asked that a priest be sent them. The prelate chose me. I'm sure he had his good reasons — for he's as cute as a fox. Though, I don't think it was my piety that recommended me to him so much as a certain right hook that I landed on a sinner of my parish. You see, to the bishop the West is a place where a man counts himself lucky to make it through to lunch without being Bowie-knifed. Just the place for a ruffian like me, in fact.'

The priest laid bacon strips on a pan. As they were beginning to sizzle, Tillet heard a throaty moan come from behind the canvas cover of the wagon.

A small boot appeared and a slim, black-stockinged calf, then another, then a girl with a heavy mass of gleaming black hair lowered herself from the back of the wagon to the ground. She stood with her weight thrown on one foot and took her time over a luxurious yawn. As she stretched her arms her blouse pulled taut over her small, pointed breasts.

Father Slattery frowned. 'So you're awake at last, you sleepy-headed devil.'

The black-haired girl opened her drowsy eyes. They seemed to take a long time to focus. Finally she appeared to notice Day and Tillet and said, 'Ah, we have guests to dinner.' Her Mexican accent was strong and breathy. It sounded like, ' . . . hests to theenar'. Her little, sharp-looking teeth were strikingly white against the red of her lips and her skin was the colour of coffee made with cream.

Tillet felt himself being nudged and looked to see the edge of a tin plate prodding his elbow. The blonde girl's eyes had lost something of their softness.

The priest's good humour seemed to have deserted him. They ate in silence until Day said, 'You see a rider on a white horse come by?'

The priest's eyes narrowed. 'Yes, a long individual, on a white stallion. Dressed for a funeral.'

'That's him. He's been riding ahead of us all morning. We've tried to hail him a couple of times, but he don't answer. And then, when I put on a sprint and tried to catch up with him, dogged if he don't disappear, like he'd snuck into the woods to hide or something.'

'Yes, a queer-looking bird. He stopped over there. Gave a good hard look in our direction. I must say, I didn't like the look of that fellow.'

The blonde girl forgot her shyness and blurted out, 'Neither did I like the look of him. When he turned his back I did this.' She made a gesture with her right hand. Her first finger and her little finger stuck out of her bunched fist.

'Ah, the evil eye,' the priest said. 'Oh well, if I was allowed to believe in that sort of thing, I'd agree with you. If anyone ever had it, that one did.'

Tillet asked, 'What's the evil eye?'

'Oh, it's a European superstition. They believe some people can make a milk-cow dry up, make a mother miscarry . . . ' He repeated the gesture the girl had made. 'This is supposed to ward it off.'

'What he look like?' The dark girl's voice had lost its sleepy drawl and become hard and tense. To Tillet it seemed the blood had drained from her cheeks.

The priest looked at her in surprise for a moment, then replied, 'Well, he was tall and thin, as I said. From one of the Latin countries, by the cast of him, but of the pure Spanish type — that's to say, no Indian or Negro blood, but perhaps more than a dash of the Moor.

Carried himself like a don — but what is it, child? Do you know him?'

The dark girl seemed to gather herself with an effort. 'No I never see him before.' She began to chew slowly and carefully on her meat, her face expressionless.

'I was wondering,' Day said, 'could we sleep by your fire tonight, Reverend?'

The priest looked doubtful

'You can trust us,' Day pressed.

The priest met Tillet's eye and whatever he saw there must have reassured him. 'Well, and why not then? An old man gets mistrustful, but as far as I can judge you're both decent lads.'

3

The girls slept inside the wagon while the priest rolled up in his blanket and slept underneath. The boys had no bedding, so they lay down by the fire. They heaped a stack of brush and deadwood beside it so that if the cold woke them in the night they could build up the blaze again.

Tillet lay awake. His mind was on the Mexican girl and the look she'd given him through the opening in the canvas of the wagon as he'd walked along behind. It was sleepy and a little amused. It had seemed to share some secret with him.

The other girl was pretty too. The sun made a halo of her golden hair as she sat up on the front of the wagon. She looked fresh and part of the morning and his heart became calm when he looked at her. The dark girl disturbed him, but he found himself waiting for a glimpse of her through the opening in the canvas of the wagon.

Sometime in the night Tillet woke to the sound of whispers. He recognized the Mexican girl's voice. He lay, afraid to move a muscle, and listened to her and Day murmuring. A sad, heavy weight pressed on his heart.

The girl said, 'Is your friend awake?'

His first impulse was to pretend to be asleep, but he murmured, 'Don't mind me. I reckon I'll take a walk.'

'No, I want to talk with both of you.'

'Oh, well now,' Day sounded disgruntled. 'Why don't we wake the other two and have a hoe-down?'

'Shh! I just want to talk with you. Do not make a mistake about me. I am no saint, but I am not a whore either. I stick with one man. And I got a man. Something happen and we broke up, but I'm going back to him now.'

'He in Lodestar?'

'No, I ask to go with the priest

because Lodestar is in my direction. But I leave him tomorrow and go up in the pine woods. Why don't you come with me — both of you?'

'Yeah. I can see how you'd want to have an escort up into the hills, but what's in it for us?'

'I could get Dave to make you a part of his operation. Dave catches horses. You could make some money. Some good money. But I got to tell you now — some of the horses he catches have been caught once already.'

'You mean rustling?' Day sounded interested.

'I never aimed to step outside the law,' Tillet said.

'Hell, we're rustlers already. We took Pa's horse, didn't we?'

'Yeah, but . . . '

'Listen to me.' There was an edge to Dolores' voice, a note of ferocity. 'One thing I know about this world — you got to have the guts to take what you need. Look . . . '

She laid her hand on her breast and

27

gathered the material of her blouse between finger and thumb. 'This is silk — eh — nice? It feels good. Do you think I was born wearing silk? Well, I tell you — I wore dresses made out of flour sacks. No, I was just like you. Your shirt, Johnny, it is worn thin like cigarette paper. And you, Day, I can still smell the farmyard dung offa your sod-buster boots. So, are you gonna stay poor and miserable all your life? Break your back for ten cents an hour? Scratch at the dirt until it become so you can never scrub the black rim offa your fingernails? Or have you got the nerve to take your fair share?'

The firelight gleamed on the whites of Dolores' eyes as her glance darted from one to the other. Her face was set, the top lip slightly curled back from her teeth. Day and Tillet stared into the fire. Tillet watched a little square of white ash peel off a branch and ride up a flame until the flame dropped it and left it to the wind.

Dolores rose to her feet. 'OK, think

about it. Sleep on it. But remember — if you want something in this life, you gotta have the guts to take it for yourself.'

After a couple of hours' travelling the next morning, they came to a divide in the road. They were on high ground now. The land to the south and east continued to rise, and pine trees bristled against the sky there.

Day halted the horse and dismounted. 'This is where we part company, Reverend.' He motioned to Dolores, who climbed down from the wagon. 'Come and jump on the horse.'

The priest gave them a long look. 'So, you're going up in the hills, Dolores? I don't need to ask why. I heard you talking last night. And you're going up with her, young fellow?' The priest turned to Tillet. 'And what is your choice? You strike me as a decent lad. We could find you an honest job in Lodestar.'

Day grinned with one side of his mouth. 'Bustin' sod.'

'He's built for it. Fine solid back to him. It's not everyone that's got what it takes for farming. God gave you a strong body, John. You should not be ashamed to use it for honest toil.'

Day gave Tillet a level look. 'You're a good friend, Johnny, but I made up my mind and I'm going up in the hills.' The edge left his voice. 'Come on with us, partner.'

Day turned and made a stirrup of his hands for Dolores. Instead, she walked over to Tillet. She came close enough for him to smell her. He felt her feathery touch against him. Her eyes seemed to let him see all the things she kept hidden from everyone else. 'Don't let them crush your spirit, Johnny. Come with us and be free.'

She turned slowly and walked away, her shoulders hunched and defeated.

The priest picked up the reins with a sigh and said, 'Well, let's be going if we're going.'

Tillet blurted out, 'I ain't coming.'

The priest let the reins down slowly

and sat with his eyes lowered and his mouth twisted down in disappointment.

'So long, Father. Goodbye. Anna.'

Anna had flushed red and her eyelids fluttered over her lowered eyes. She seemed unable to look at him or answer. She gave a jerky nod of farewell.

Tillet stared at her and then, with a feeling of blanking his mind and taking a high dive into a pool, he turned and ran down the left fork of the trail.

4

Up in the hills, hemmed round by pine-trees, a dead-ended gulch widened into a flat hollow before a fall in the old river-bed brought its sandstone walls crowding in again. When the narrow exit was blocked off with pine saplings it formed a natural corral, and it was here that Dave Harper and his men kept the horses they rounded up in their forays along the Trinity River.

Harper had a dark, gypsy face that looked hard as granite. He looked Day and Tillet over doubtfully, but when Dolores spoke to him coaxingly his face softened into a smile. The tender expression appeared a little absurd on a tough face like his. He told them he would give them a chance. That very night, in fact. The sutler who traded Harper's horses with the Mexican government was pressing him for a big consignment fast, and Harper had decided to make a raid on the next valley where a herd of mustangs was being bred with imported studs. It was not a good thing to work so close to home, but they were going to chance it to make up their numbers before the vaqueros arrived to drive the animals south.

Day and Tillet were furnished with fast mounts and weapons. Day now carried two six-guns stuck in his belt. He did not show any sign of the nervousness that Tillet felt. He made friends quickly with the men, keeping up a banter with them as they rode. Even Dave Harper's face showed a grudging smile.

They left the pine woods behind and came down into a valley. A full moon rode high in an empty sky and shed a light that was almost as clear as day over the sparsely treed grassland through which a river made a slow curve. The dark spread of the ranch buildings was visible down at the bend of the valley and near it an acre was corralled off.

When they reached the corral, one of Harper's men, a little fellow with the look of a half-wit, climbed in among the animals. He seemed to have a way with horses. He singled out a big stallion and went to work befriending it, making low cooing noises and feeding it lumps of sugar. The horses followed the big stallion out of the corral with hardly a sound.

Half a mile from the ranch, they seemed to realize they were free and began to gallop for the hills. They led them a hard chase before a steep slope took the steam out of them and they fell away to a walk. Tillet's mount was breathing hard and working up a lather by now.

No one had spoken since the chase began, but now Tillet heard someone shout, 'Hey, Dave.' The freckle-faced boy they called Abilene was pointing up ahead. Tillet looked and saw a rider on a white horse profiled against the sky up on the ridge of the valley. Harper reined his horse to a halt.

'Ain't that the character we saw on the trail?' Day said. 'The skinny devil — on the white horse — remember?'

'You know that guy?' Harper's voice was hard and abrupt. 'What does he want?'

'We don't know him.'

The rider was a dead, black silhouette against the star-filled sky, but the horse gave back the brilliance of the starlight as a pale lustre.

A flame appeared to burst from the dark figure's head. There was a smack, like a strap striking wood, and Harper's head snapped back on his neck. It bounced forward again. Then he was sliding out of his saddle, hitting Tillet's horse which side-stepped out of the way. He landed face up and Tillet saw there was a hole punched in his right temple.

There was an ear-splitting blast as of a cannon going off next to Tillet's ear and he was engulfed in the stench of powder-smoke. Then the valley itself seemed to explode around him as Harper's men blazed at the rider on the white horse. By the time they had holstered their pistols as useless and were pulling out their rifles, he was already over the rise.

'Dave's dead. Blew out his brains.'

'The damn' horses!' The man who wore the long hair and buckskins of a scout began to spur his horse back down into the valley. 'I ain't letting fifty good head of horse get away.'

One and then another and then all of them, Day and Tillet in their midst, began to chase after the herd.

Tillet saw Day up ahead pointing, stabbing with his finger and screaming something. He looked and saw a gleam of light amongst the ranch buildings.

'We've woken the ranch!'

Now little black shapes like roaches could be seen scuttling out of the shadows of the ranch buildings.

They had to dig hard with their spurs

to urge their horses back up the steep uneven slope.

'They're near on our tails. My God, they'll catch us.'

'They ain't caught us yet.' Day let out a yell of defiance, and Tillet saw him pulling ahead. His animal's neck was stretched out, its head almost touching the slope.

When Tillet stole a glance back, his heart jolted with fright to see how close they were. He lashed at his horse's neck with the ends of his reins and stabbed his spurs into its sides. Its head pistoned as it flung itself at the gradient.

The slope began to lessen and the horses picked up speed. They ploughed through tall fern and then came on to a beaten track. The trail they followed wound down out of the hills and their horses flew along it in ground-swallowing bounds. Scrub glided by on either side. Then the ground fell away to the right so that the tops of the trees were below them.

An outcrop of granite broke through the scrub. A trail had been blasted through it and its rubble strewed the slope. The trail made a narrow turn around the outcrop and Tillet leaned hard in and dashed around it. He glimpsed a white blob ahead. A second glimpse past the riders in front showed it was a wagon's canvas gleaming in the moonlight.

Day slid through the narrow channel between the side of the wagon and the granite wall. The little half-wit wheeled nimbly into the opening after him. Sparks spurted as a hoof struck bare rock. The one called Murdoch tried to pass on the outside. His horse went off the narrow trail and Tillet saw it running and sliding down the slope, trying to dodge the boulders of granite and the scrub.

As Tillet passed the wagon he had to pull up his leg to stop it being crushed against the wheel. His spur raked the back of the inside horse. He looked back and saw the team rearing and glimpsed the silver hair of the priest as he stood up fighting to control it.

Tillet looked back again. The team was running. They were past the granite wall. The trail had widened but still the team held to the outside of it. Then the outside horse dipped, seemed to go down on its knee. The inside was wrenched to the right and both ran off the track. Tillet saw the wagon begin to turn over before it disappeared.

He wheeled round through a patch of gorse and leaned back on the reins so that the horse's front legs rose up and pawed the air. In the confusion of his mind it seemed they'd all been acting like kids playing tag and now something serious had happened. The broken-nosed cowboy and the freckle-faced kid almost ran him down as he jumped to the ground. The horse didn't want to follow him down the slope, but he couldn't leave it up on top to give him away. He hauled at it with all the strength of his back and it began to pick its way down.

It lost its footing, went down on its side and began to slide down the loose dirt. Tillet slid after it until the slope began to level and he was able to dig his feet into the dirt.

The wagon was tilted up at an angle with its back jammed in a clump of scrub and brush. The priest lay half-a-dozen yards from it. As he turned him over, his eyes opened slightly but only showed the whites.

He went to the wagon and climbed on the haunch of one of the horses. It neighed in pain and wrenched its head around trying to bite him. Inside he could only make out dark shapes under the white glow of the canvas. He felt his way through the mess of objects and found the girl huddled against the backboard. He prodded her but she gave no sign of life.

He felt something was called for from him, but he did not know what to do. He just sat there with his heart thudding and his hands trembling. Even when he heard voices above him, he continued to sit there frozen.

A shadow appeared against the canvas: and a blade punched through and began to rip it down. The vague outline of a head came through the opening and a voice said, 'Take it easy now. You hurt?'

'I'm all right, but there's a girl hurt bad in here.'

The man drew back through the slit and called, 'Somebody hurt bad in the prairie-schooner.'

They made bowlines out of their ropes and hauled the priest and the girl up. A hand helped Tillet up on to the path and a voice said, 'It's all right. They're both alive and you're in good shape. Come on over to the boss, son. He's a real British sir, you know. But being how this is America, we just call him Mr Gabriel.'

The man was mounted on a pure blood horse of a breed Tillet had never seen before. He sat easily in the saddle, but without the western slouch. When he spoke, his voice was clear, every word as flawless as a newly stamped silver coin.

'Is this your wagon?'

'Yeah . . . well, I was travelling in it.'

With a slight motion of his head, the man indicated Tillet's horse, which had been hauled back up on to the path. 'And the horse?'

'The horse . . . yeah, that's my horse. I was riding with them, 'longside of the wagon. These bunch of riders come — '

A whining drawl interrupted him. 'One of them bad men was mounted on a piebald — and I reckon this is the same fella.'

Tillet stared up dumbly at the man on the thoroughbred. He could not see his eyes. His face was in shadow, outlined by the pale gleam of his hair. The man looked away and said, 'How are they?'

'The preacher, he's OK. Gonna have a pigeon egg on his head, I guess. The girl, she busted up her leg.'

A voice called from below. 'Charley, tell the boss I'm gonna let off a shot. One of the horses broke its back.'

Seconds later the blast of a gun sounded.

'The other's OK. If you throw down some ropes we could haul her up and the wagon as well.'

One of them, who stood coiling a rope, jerked his head at Tillet. 'What about him, boss?'

The man turned to Tillet again. 'What is your name?'

'John Tillet.'

'And your occupation?'

'Thief,' someone said. There was a murmur of agreement.

'What do you say?' the man asked.

Tillet remained silent.

The man with the rope said, 'He ain't got the nerve to deny it.' He came up to Tillet and slung a loop over his shoulders. Then he looked up at the man on the thoroughbred, who nodded. The rope was jerked tight at his elbows. They led over his horse, fitted his foot in the stirrup and began to push him up.

A voice rang out. 'Leave him go!'

Tillet dropped back to the ground. He turned and saw Day.

'Didn't think I'd leave you to it, Johnny?' Day sat his horse, brandishing a pistol in each hand. His eyes were burning brightly. 'Step over here, partner.'

When he moved, Tillet was jerked back by the rope.

'Leave him go, I said. I'm warning you.' Day's fingers opened and closed on the handles of his Colts. 'You, from the way you're sitting there like the king of the Prussians, I guess you're the boss of this crew. If you don't let my partner go, I'm gonna put holes in you.'

The man on the thoroughbred just gazed steadily at Day. Day gave his pistols a threatening shake. A wild glitter came into his eyes.

Tillet saw the rope open over Day's head. The loop seemed to spread lazily,

44

but even as he called out a warning it dropped and cinched tight and Day was jerked out of his saddle. One of the guns exploded and then it seemed that half-a-dozen men dived on him as one.

5

Ahead of them the wagon, with the priest and the girl still unconscious in the back, drew away, its torn canvas fluttering. When they reached the bed of the valley, they bore away from the direction of the ranch-house. They splashed across the river which shone like a silver road curving up into the hills.

Day, his arms tied to his waist, turned awkwardly in the saddle. His face was a pale blob in the moonlight.

'This ain't the way to the ranch. Where're we bound?'

A whining drawl answered, 'Why, you're Hell-bound.'

The breath hitched in Tillet's wind-pipe. They rode on in silence broken by the jingle of harness and the swish of the animals' legs stepping through the long grass.

'Johnny . . . the bastards are going to hang us without a trial. For the sake of a few miserable nags . . . can you believe it?'

All Tillet could think of was that he'd only turned eighteen.

'If I had my brace of guns I'd show you boys what.'

No one answered. In the silence and the moon-light things seemed unreal. Tillet felt he couldn't grasp what was going on. A big mistake was happening, and it was carrying him along with it without giving him time to work out an explanation.

An isolated clump of cottonwoods rose up out of the grass ahead, and he knew that was where it ended.

'You dirty bastards! You ain't got the sand to fight me. I'd lick any one of you in fair fight.' Day's shouts echoed forlornly from the walls of the valley.

Somebody began to sing a lament. He sang it quietly, the way a cowboy does to soothe his nervous cattle, but the high nasal voice sounded as clear as the peal of a distant bell.

Tillet felt the chill of death creep into his heart. They would bury them on the open range, and in the spring the grass would cover the bare sod of their graves so that no one could even tell where they lay.

The singing stopped. A hand halted his horse beneath a tall cottonwood with spreading branches. With the horses motionless there was no longer a sound and the silence of the range came rushing in like the breath of eternity sweeping across the grass.

Strange thoughts were going through his mind. It came to him that he could feel the weight of the earth. It was unbelievably heavy. And it was real. The only real thing. And when it was gone there was nothing. He wanted them to get it over. His mind was reeling with these thoughts. But no one would do anything. No one would even say anything. Except, someone was crying.

'Please don't kill me, men,' Day pleaded.

The man on the thoroughbred rode up and sat motionless, a dark shape outlined against millions of winking stars. He nodded his head.

Two hands threw their lariats over the same thick limb of the tree. Tillet's hat was pulled off. The touch of the rope on his shoulders made him jump as though burnt. His heart was thudding against his ribs and his jaws were clenched so hard it felt like a band of steel were tightening round his head. Day began to struggle wildly as they put the rope on him.

He was crying, 'No, don't kill me. Don't kill me.'

Finally they managed to work the rope over his head. The nooses were pulled tight. Tillet's brain clouded and the man on the thoroughbred faded from before his eyes.

'Please don't hang me, mister,' Day sobbed like a broken-hearted child.

Tillet squeezed his eyes shut.

A voice yelled.

The horse leapt forward and bucked as his spurs raked it. His lungs tried to gasp air as he swung back, but they couldn't. His feet thrashed and tried to find a purchase on thin air, but nothing could lessen the dead weight pulling on his neck. His brain showered thoughts like sparks from a grinding-wheel, and even now he was casting around crazily for some plan of escape.

A voice thudded in his brain. The thudding was going to burst his eyeballs. All at once he felt as light as a wisp of smoke and he thought his soul must be flying to Heaven.

'You'll be all right,' somebody told him. He found he was sitting with his back propped against the bole of the tree. Day was sitting beside him. A ranch-hand was slapping his face and he was coming round.

Above them, the clear silvery voice of the Englishman spoke. 'The customs of the frontier have their rough-and-ready charm, but I'm afraid I find the lynch party a little too quaint for my taste. And then, I cannot agree that any creature that walks the earth on four legs is worth the life of a man.'

One of the hands spoke. 'I think you're wrong, boss. It ain't just a case of your horses. People out these parts got to know that rustlin' means hangin', and that's that.'

'They know what hanging means. Let them live to profit by the knowledge.' He turned and looked down on them. Tillett could only see a dark shadow and a pale crown of hair against the stars. 'I've given you back your lives. It's up to you what you do with them.'

★ ★ ★

The coming days were bad ones for both of them. At first they spoke about what had happened and tried to make light of it but, as the days passed, they grew silent and avoided each other's eyes. Tillet felt a numbness

51

come over him. He drifted through the days barely thinking. Day brooded. If he opened his mouth it was to throw out something short and vicious. One evening he started a fight over the food that one of the ranch-hands had left them.

'How come you got more pork to your beans than me?' Day demanded, after Tillet had handed him his dish.

'They just the same, Day,' he told him.

Day's stare was sullen. 'You hogged the best for yourself.'

'God damn,' said Tillet. 'Take mine.' He grabbed Day's plate and shoved his own into his hands. He stuck a spoonful of beans into his mouth and scalded himself.

Day flung his plate away and jumped to his feet.

'You hogged the best. You figure you're more man than me, so you're entitled to the lion's share, that it?'

'You're crazy.'

'You think you're more man than

me, that it? I guess you think I ain't nothing but a blubbin' baby so I don't deserve no man's share of grub. That the way you're figurin'? You puke-lickin' dog, I'll show you who's the better man. Stand and fight.'

'I don't want to fight you, Day. You're acting crazy. I was as scared as you when they strung us up.'

Tillet had to put down his plate and scramble to his feet when Day rushed him.

He couldn't bring himself to fight to win. The way Day was now, he felt, a licking would knock the rest of the heart out of him. It would finish them as friends, and he didn't want that.

Tillet took the beating, but it made no difference anyway. Day packed his half of the food and rode back the way they had come.

6

He heard the distant sound of axes pecking at the pines and later the whine of a flutter-wheel told him that a logging company must be working in the hills. On the way down out of the hills he passed some abandoned cabins and excavations, then the trail began to flatten out and he came to a crossroads.

According to the weatherbeaten Wells Fargo sign, Dunn's Staging Post lay to the west. The left-hand road would bring him to a town called Redemption. The trail straight ahead, that Tillet chose, led to Lodestar.

It was little more than a main street, with a store called Caldwell's, a saloon with the same name, a stage depot, and a few workshops and shacks. The couple of people he saw, a tailor and a blacksmith standing outside their neighbouring shops, gave him a sideways look and no greeting. From the other end of town sounds of sawing and hammering came and Tillet followed them till he found a group of men busy building.

The priest was bent over a two-by-four stud hard at work with a saw. He glanced up and noticed Tillet, gave another few strokes of the saw and then stopped.

'Well, lad, we meet again after all.'

The priest left his saw wedged in the cut and settled himself on the trestle while Tillet dismounted. 'By God, every priest should have to build his own church. There are too many fat black crows on the eastern seaboard.'

Tillet said, 'You're hurt, Father.'

The priest touched the side of his face which was scraped and scabbed over. 'Oh, yes . . . had a little mishap on the road. I'll live though.'

'Anna — is — was she hurt too?'

'I'm afraid she was, poor girl. Her leg was broken in a couple of places.'

'Will she be all right?'

The priest eyed Tillet before answering. 'I guess it's too early to tell yet.' He took up the saw and cut off the end of the two-by-four. 'What next, Karl?'

A big blond man — most of this group were fair, Tillet noticed — called back, 'Eight foot and six inch, Father.'

'Yes, let's pray to God,' said the priest as he measured a timber with a folding rule. 'It would be a shame if she ended up with a limp.'

'Can I — need a hand?' Tillet nodded towards the construction. Two large stud walls were already completed and were stacked flat on the ground.

He borrowed a hammer and went to work with them. They were sure and steady in their work, not rushing and never slacking. When they spoke to each other they seemed on the point of losing their temper. But he supposed this must be just their German accent. They sounded the same way when they were smiling. When a rest was called, another panel of the church's walls had been nailed together.

As they drank bottles of beer and ate smoked sausage with bread, the priest introduced him to the rest of the men. They shook his hand and said carefully, 'How do you do?' It must have been the English greeting they had all learned. 'And Karl here is Anna's uncle,' the priest told him.

'My brother Heinrich decided to spend her dowry on a passage to America for her,' Karl explained. He twisted his mouth and said with a touch of bitterness, 'Germany — there is nothing there for a poor man. And this great Bismarck that all shout about — 'Every man should smoke ten thousand cigars before he dies', he says.' He shook his head. 'Let the sly old devils play chess with Europe. America is young and simple, and a man can work and live here.'

'Yes, America's a fine country and full of possibility,' agreed the priest. 'And who knows but that the town of Lodestar won't end up as glorious as

57

Munich or Amsterdam in the time to come.'

Karl's slightly bulbous eyes glanced up into the town. 'I am afraid that Lodestar is starting badly.'

'It's true that some of its residents are not of the most savoury. Ah, I'll not let that put me off. Old Nick knows me well by now. He can be sure of a good scrap off Slattery. There's more than one soul I've pulled by the scruff of the neck on to the path of salvation.'

'I think it is better to leave them alone,' Karl said. 'Lodestar welcomes criminals. Once, Wolf and Gerhardt went into the saloon and they saw a man drinking whiskey underneath where his own Wanted-poster was stuck to the wall. They were lucky to get out of there. They started to tease them, making jokes about Germans. They wanted to start a fight.'

'I cannot fight,' said a fat man with mournful eyes.

'And if you could, do you think that would have mattered?' demanded Karl in a stern tone. 'I tell you everyone in that place would have taken their turn to kick you on the ground.'

'I regret that day more than any other of my life.' The man who spoke was big and raw-boned. His jaw was set hard and his eyes were cold and sullen.

Karl glared at him. 'I say you were right, Wolf.'

'In this Texas, they only respect you if you fight. They do not respect us Germans because they think we cannot fight.'

'What are we doing with the French? Playing games of tennis? The French, whom everyone thinks are the best fighters in the world, and we Germans have them running.'

'And so next week they will have us running.' Karl looked contemptuously over his shoulder. 'We came here to get away from that stupidity.'

'At least back there they did not look at us as inferiors. In this Texas if you are not English, Scotch or Irish, you might as well be a red man.'

'Now, I don't think they welcome the Irish very much either,' said the priest.

'But there are many people from Ireland here,' objected Karl.

'From Ulster. The people of that part are not flattered if you call them Irish. Their blood is Scottish and their religion is Luther's.'

'My ma was from Ulster, and she sure didn't like the Irish,' Tillet said. 'Pa was too, but he never had a bad word for nobody.'

'Well he sounds like a good Christian then,' the priest said. 'German and Irish, it will be our task to show the proud Texan that we are Christians and hard workers and every bit as good as they.'

'Better than they.'

'And so the circle again begins.' Karl raised his bottle before him. 'Let it be 'Good Americans' and I will drink to it.'

In the late afternoon, Tillet rode

out with them under a sky piled high with golden clouds. Along the bottom lands of the river, emerald cornfields rippled in the breeze. Tillet, raised a ploughboy, could smell the richness of the dirt. At the third farm they said goodbye to the rest and the priest, Karl and Tillet turned down a path that led to a new two-storey house. As he followed the priest and Karl up the porch-steps Tillet admired how well built it was. The boards were wedged tight and the uprights all lined up perfectly one behind the other.

Karl's wife met them at the door with a welcoming smile and said, 'How do you do?' to Tillet. Inside, Anna sat at a table by the window hemming curtains. Tillet caught a glimpse of her startled eyes before she ducked down over her stitching. He saw that her right leg stuck out stiffly in front of her.

The golden evening light lingered in the room as they ate supper. Tillet had never imagined that a house could be so neat and spotless. Pictures and painted plates hung on the walls and little plaster ornaments covered the mantelpiece. A grandfather clock marked the quarter-hours with a peaceful chime. The food was the best he had ever tasted. Tillet felt happy but a little uncomfortable. He felt the lack of his own upbringing among these gentle-mannered golden-haired people. His family had been religious and law-abiding enough, but it had never been thought of as respectable.

While the priest and Karl chatted quietly, Anna and Mrs Miller seemed to carry on a conversation without words. He saw Anna smile shyly at Mrs Miller and then Mrs Miller glanced at him. Tillet glanced away awkwardly, embarrassed and pleased.

Eventually, the golden dusk dimmed and became grey and Karl, with a sigh, lit the lantern. Anna rose and Tillet felt the blood heat his face as he saw her limp.

Later, Karl gave her his arm and

helped her up to her room. When he returned, his face was troubled. 'She is in pain. I pray to God she gets better. I cannot bear to think of her hobbling always like that — like an old woman.'

'We'll pray to God for the child.'

'May those responsible rot in Hell.'

'Now, Karl, let's stick to praying and forget about the cursing. It is not always easy to forgive, but that is what it means to follow Christ.' The priest intoned the words as though reading a familiar lesson. Karl sighed and nodded politely, then his good nature made him soften and he forced a smile onto his lips.

★ ★ ★

'Ah, John, I'm going to like it here.' The priest gave a contented sigh as they lay in the loft of the barn listening to frogs croaking on the riverbank. 'And if I wasn't in the Lord's service — and maybe a few years younger — I believe

I would take myself a German wife. For they surely know how to cook . . . that they do . . . that they do. Irish girls can't cook worth a damn . . . '

Soon the priest's snores were mingling with the croak of the frogs, but Tillet lay awake, excluded from the peace of the night. He would leave next morning, he decided. If only he had chosen to go with the priest and the girl that day when they'd come to the parting of the road. But he hadn't. And now all he could do was travel down the road a bit further until he'd left this part of his life in the past.

* * *

Against the star-filled sky, outlines of hills and trees swung past his eyes. His tongue was too big for his mouth and his body was heavy enough to pull off his head. The rope turned slowly and now he could see Day. Day's neck was six inches long and his dark tongue poked out between his black lips. But a faint indrawn whistle of air told he was breathing. A blackbird sat on his shoulder and, as he watched, it stabbed its beak at his face.

'Leave him alone. He ain't dead yet.' His voice was only a croak. The bird paid no attention and slowly Day swung out of his sight.

The stars hung one behind the other and stretched off into the heavens in their millions. Though they filled the sky with light, the ground below was pitch dark and he could see nothing. But he could hear scuffling and grunting noises. They filled him with dread. He tried to shut his eyes, but they bulged so much that he couldn't drag the lids over them.

There was a thump as Day's body hit the ground and the branch sprang up a little. He screamed, but it came out as only a croak. He felt the darkness below was alive with movement. He knew Day was being carried away. He tried to shout that Day wasn't dead yet, but his words were only a croak past his swollen tongue.

There was a snuffling and champing above him. Hot spit fell on his head. The rope gave and the terrible weight was gone from his neck. His feet hit the ground and his body buckled on top of them. He could feel fingers like worms crawling over him and he shouted, 'Leave me alone. I ain't dead yet.'

He could smell the rotten stench of them and feel their wormy fingers all over him. They picked him up and he tried to shout, 'I ain't dead — '

'You're Hell-bound,' he heard.

He screamed at them, to make them understand he wasn't dead, but they paid no attention. They had him fast and were scurrying off with him. He screamed, 'I ain't — '

A hand was shaking him and a voice rumbled in his ear. The priest's silver hair gleamed in the moonlight streaming through the loft doors. 'You gave me a fright, John,' the priest was saying. 'Between you and that blasted frog, I thought I was below among the damned.'

A sound like the honking of a giant donkey was coming from somewhere outside.

'I guess I was dreaming. I'm all right.'

'Are you? I've been watching you today. You don't seem all right to me.'

'I am,' Tillet said flatly. 'I said I was sorry.'

The priest did not give up easily. 'I'd say your mind was giving you pain. That's all right. A man feels pain, even when his belly's full and he's safe from harm. God will send you more pain before He calls you to your reward. But He'll send you help too. I'm here to help, if you'll let me.'

Tillet began talking. 'Me and Day, we got ourselves into some trouble . . . '

The priest moved back and sat against the frame of the loft opening so that his face was in darkness and only his hair shone bright in the moonlight. He said quietly, 'Go on.'

'We broke the law. Got caught. They . . . hanged us.'

The frog began honking again. When it stopped and Tillet remained silent, the priest said, 'So, am I talking to a ghost?'

'Might as well be, I reckon. Feels like my heart and guts have been scooped out clean. They cut us down. They were just trying to throw a scare in us. It was too much for me, though. I guess they broke me, and that's it.'

'I've never faced death myself. But I've seen lads go to the wars — stalwart lads and dreadful proud of their scarlet coats. And I've seen some of them come shuffling home with their backs bowed. I've seen people broken, in their hearts or minds, and some have withered and died between a spring and an autumn. 'Tis a great pity . . . a great pity.' The priest shook his head and sighed. 'But I've seen broken spirits mend like broken bones, also. Have faith, John. Have faith in the mercy of our Saviour.'

A loud honking broke the peace of the night again. When it stopped, the priest continued, 'You are among good people now. You can rest here. Rest and let your mind heal up.'

'I can't stay here.'

'And why not? What you said was between you and me. You broke the law, but you've paid for it. It was only a lapse and no one need ever know about it.'

'Anna, she might have to limp for the rest of her life. That's my fault. Remember the bunch of riders that passed you in the mountains?'

'Yes, I guessed you were among them when you mentioned the hanging. That Englishman, he told us how he'd caught two of the thieves and how he served them.'

'It was me who scared your team. So I'm — '

'You didn't mean to; it was an accident. And you came back to try and help. Let your remorse settle the debt. For my part, I forgive you outright. And Anna . . . she's an exceptional girl — '

'I can't tell her.'

'If you don't tell her, she can't forgive you. I . . . I think I know how she feels about you. If you can't find an answer to that feeling then perhaps you had better leave. But if you can — then throw yourself on her mercy. The Millers, they are decent, law-abiding folk. There is no need to say anything to them for now. Let them get to know you and see that you are as decent and hard-working as themselves. You are young and you are on your own, John. There are so many traps and pitfalls in the world. So many ways to go wrong. Stay among these good people. There is a home for you here.'

7

'Wait. I come with you. I want to get a plane-iron.'

Wolf climbed up on the wagon beside Tillet. His face looked tense and white.

'I can get it for you. if you give me the money. A jack-plane?'

'I want to choose,' Wolf said shortly.

Tillet, a little nettled by Wolf's manner, said nothing further. He whistled and started the team.

The blacksmith and the tailor were sitting on either side of the dead stove in Caldwell's store. The blacksmith had an indulgent grin on his big, flat face. The little tailor was chafing him, but keeping a wary eye out at the same time to see how he was taking it. At the counter, Caldwell and another man were conversing in low tones. They all broke off and

71

turned their eyes on Tillet and Wolf: the little tailor's bloodstreaked yellow, glittering with daring and apprehension; the blacksmith's slow and arrogant; the man at the counter's savage but wary, the eyes of a man permanently at bay; Caldwell's sure and hooded. Their eyes appraised Tillet and Wolf for a second and then dismissed them as though not worth any more attention.

Caldwell had a dead butt stuck to his lower lip. His voice was slow and drowsy. Tillet glanced up at him sharply when he told him twenty dollars as the price of a keg of nails, but Caldwell's hooded eyes turned away slowly and insolently as he resumed his conversation.

It was daylight robbery, thought Tillet as he dumped the keg on the back of the wagon. But if you didn't buy at Caldwell's you went without, it seemed. As he stepped back into the store, he heard Wolf saying with heavy sarcasm, 'How much you want for this? Fifty dollar?'

72

'Five'll do,' Caldwell said.

Wolf flapped the plane-iron in his hand. 'Five dollar,' he repeated, drawing the words out. His face was chalky but his eyes were sullen and determined. 'My friend, I give you one-fifty for this because it ain't made of gold.'

Caldwell unpeeled the butt from his lip. 'You give me five dollars if you want that thing, *amigo*.'

Wolf kept flapping the plane-iron rapidly in his hand. Tillet could see the recklessness building in him. He said, 'Let's go, Wolf. Leave the iron.'

Caldwell turned back and continued his chat. The other man kept darting glances at Wolf, but Caldwell acted as though he didn't exist and kept his voice to the low drone he'd been using before.

The porch boards clattered and another customer appeared in the doorway. He wore a suit, but no necktie, and his waistcoat was unbuttoned. He cast a bright-eyed, inquisitive look around the store, seemed to find some quiet amusement in what he saw, and walked up to the counter where he selected a cigar from the humidor. 'Howdy, Luke.'

Caldwell gave him a friendly nod. 'Howdy, Doc.'

The newcomer dropped a coin on the table and went over to the stove where the blacksmith and the tailor were sitting in frozen attitudes watching Wolf out of the corners of their eyes.

The plane-iron stopped flapping in Wolf's hand. Tillet was about to go to him when Wolf stormed over to the counter and snatched a cigar out of the humidor. 'How much for this?'

'Dollar,' said Caldwell, without looking at him.

'One dollar.' Wolf flung the cigar on the counter. 'For him, a quarter, for me one dollar it costs?'

'Doc, is Marty over in the bar?'

'Sure is, Luke.'

Caldwell muttered something to the man at the counter, who nodded and went out the door.

Wolf dived into his pocket and pulled out some notes. He fumbled away two of them, dropped one, snatched it from the floor and flung them on the counter. 'For this plane-iron two dollars I will pay — which still is too much.'

'Maybe you don't know how we do things in Texas, friend. I say the price and if you don't like it you leave it.'

'I know how it is in Texas, all right. You think you are the greatest in the world and you can treat everyone else like dirt. Well I am not dirt, and I am going to take this plane-iron for a fair price, and if any Texan wants to stop me, let them try. Because now I'm just in the mood.'

Wolf glared at the blacksmith who sat pale-faced and motionless, his eyes hidden behind his narrowed lids. A clattering had sounded on the boards outside while he spoke and Tillet turned to see the man who had just left was back and with him a red-haired man in a red silk vest and a snowy shirt with black armlets holding up the sleeves.

He was shortish, square, solid in the chest and shoulders. He wore gold rings on the fingers of both hands. His eyes were bright and hard.

When the man spoke his tight lips barely moved. 'What's the trouble, Dutch?'

'Ain't no trouble,' said Tillet. 'We're on our way.'

Marty turned his gaze on Tillet and looked him up and down once. 'No you ain't.'

Caldwell spoke in an easy-going, reasonable tone. 'I reckon we can let the kid off, Marty.' He looked Tillet over with his lazy eyes. 'You sound like a quiet kid, and you're a Texan. What're you doing with that bunch? You ain't a fish-eater, are you?'

'You a fish-eater?' Marty repeated.

'I'm Presbyterian,' Tillet said.

'Yeah,' said Caldwell. 'The kid wasn't causing no trouble. This here fish-eatin' Dutcher comes in and starts laying down the law to Texans, squaring up to all and sundry and

76

trying to pick a fight.'

'You trying to pick a fight, Dutch?' Marty asked.

Wolf was glaring warily at Marty. 'I don't pay no damn' five dollar for a — '

Marty let out an impatient, disgusted bark and rushed forward a few steps. Wolf retreated before him. He caught himself and stood, but when Marty feinted another charge he flinched back again.

'*Schwein!* Come!' Wolf began bellowing like a bull, his face turning purple with the effort. 'I kill you! Come!'

When Marty began to advance, Wolf threw up a boxer's guard and rushed at him. Marty dropped his head low just before they met, clinched him round the waist with his left arm and, while Wolf flailed at his back, hammered his right fist half a dozen times into his lower belly. Wolf screamed once and whirled his fists in a panicked flurry. But Marty was already out of reach and Wolf was doubling over, his mouth open as if in surprise. He staggered sideways and lurched on to the counter, knocking a glass jar on to the floor.

'God damn,' said Caldwell, as the balls of candy scattered across the floor. 'Finish it in the street.'

Four pairs of hands grabbed Wolf and manhandled him out through the door.

'OK, men,' said Marty, stepping off the porch.

The rest released Wolf and moved back. Marty stepped in and swung a fist that laid open Wolf's forehead. Blood welled up and began to pour out of the cuts. Marty, fingering his rings with his left hand, began to circle Wolf. Wolf shuffled round, trying to keep the blood out of his eyes and watch Marty. Marty skipped in and swung overhand while Wolf's knuckles were in his eyes. Wolf's left hand was knocked down and the rings raked his cheek.

Tillet, seeing Wolf's face covered

in blood, only now became aware of himself standing watching and doing nothing. He felt if he tried to help he could not do much. But it would be easier to face Wolf and the others later if he had some bruises to show. Except, it didn't look as if this was going to be a simple matter of a few bruises. Marty's eyes were hard and eager. The sight of blood seemed to please him. Once he had watched a hawk peck at a live field-mouse. The mouse made no struggle, only squeaked a little. Wolf seemed just as dazed. He felt sick and scared.

No one tried to stop him when Tillet began to run. The sheriff's office was only a few doors away. It was empty. Tillet shouted through the open door that led into the back, 'Anybody here? I need help.'

The sheriff wandered out from the back with a broom in his hand and gave Tillet a hostile stare. He wore his hair and beard after the Custer fashion. His paunchy, working-man's body did not lend itself to the dashing style.

'There's a fight outside. My friend's getting hurt bad.'

The sheriff dropped his broom in the corner and came forward in a morose saunter, forcing Tillet to jump out of his way.

'You're with them foreign sod-busters and the Irish sky-pilot, ain't you?' The sheriff leaned a hand against the sash of the window and spoke over his shoulder. 'Sausage-eaters, ain't they? That one of them rowin' with Marty? Yeah, I can tell by the blond hair. What you doing mixed up with that bunch?'

'Ain't you gonna do nothing? He's cutting him to ribbons.'

'Yeah, Marty fights in earnest when he starts.'

Tillet made for the door, but before he got to it the sheriff reached out a hand and swung it shut.

'Let me out.' Tillet pulled at the doorhandle and with his left hand tried to push the sheriff away.

'God damn you,' the sheriff swore angrily. He pulled out his gun and rapped the barrel on Tillet's ear. 'Don't you ever lay hands on me. Now you just stay right where you are; because if you go out there you're gonna get hurt.'

As Tillet watched, Wolf went down on one knee. Marty put his boot in his face and pushed him on to his back. Then he dropped to his knee and did something to Wolf. He couldn't see what, because Marty's back was to him, but he heard Wolf scream, and a yell went up from the watchers. The little tailor ran in and kicked Wolf in the hips. At that, everyone closed in on Wolf and all Tillet could see was their backs, with their legs kicking and stamping.

'They'll kill him.' Tillet had his hand on the door again, but the sheriff stuck the gun in his face and said, 'And I'll kill you if you ain't careful. Now, Marty knows what he's doing, and if he don't Luke Caldwell sure as hell does. So stay put.'

Tillet stared at the barrel of the gun and was ashamed to realize he was grateful for it. He did not want go into that bunch. And there was nothing he could do for Wolf if he did.

There was a blast of gunfire and Tillet thought they'd shot Wolf but, as the huddle of figures broke away from Wolf's body, Tillet saw they were looking down the street, and then he saw the three men ride into view. One was a fat man. The eye-patch he wore gave him a wild, disreputable look. The youngest of them was slim, straight-shouldered and carried himself as though he were used to better clothes than the range outfit he wore. The one in the middle who held the gun carried himself in the typical Texan slouch, but there was something in his manner that made it plain he was the leader of the three.

Tillet caught a glimpse of the bloody mask of Wolf's face. The sheriff had forgotten about Tillet. He stood tugging at his wiry spade beard, his eyes glued to the scene outside. Tillet pulled open the door and ran out.

The fat man was down on one knee beside Wolf.

'Is he dead?'

The fat man turned his one eye on Tillet. He looked him over for a second before saying, 'He's everything else but.'

'What's going on here?' The sheriff came striding up with his beefy shoulders swinging and a hand resting on his holstered gun. 'Put up the pistol, mister,' he said to the rider who had let off the shot, but the man kept it in his hand.

'Man came into the store and started a fight, Sheriff,' Caldwell said. 'He was asking for it, but I guess the boys got a little carried away, and it's a good job these fellows came along to stop things when they did.'

'I tried to get the sheriff but he

wouldn't come,' Tillet said to the man with the gun.

'The kid was so fired up I couldn't make out what he was saying. Well, I'm here now. And you can put the gun up, mister.'

The man on the horse still held on to the gun.

'Is there a doc in town?' the fat man asked the tailor.

The tailor pointed at the doctor, who stood panting with the exertion of kicking Wolf.

The fat man, his paunch jiggling, strode up to the doctor and slapped him hard in the face.

'Just who do you guys think you are?' The sheriff's voice was loud and deep, but sounded hollow, like the bark of a frightened dog.

'We're the law of Texas, mister,' said the fat man. 'The Texas Rangers is who we are.'

'Let's get this man off the street and set this here doctor to work on him.' The man on the horse nodded contemptuously to where the doctor stood with a hand trembling on his face.

'It was a ruby ring that put one of my lights out,' said the fat man, running his eye up and down Marty.

'Tell your friend to put up his gun and I'll put out the other, Fat.' Marty was fingering his rings and staring levelly back.

'Nate, put up the gun.'

'Let him live, Cannibal.'

The young Ranger took one of Wolf's legs and Tillet the other while the man called Cannibal lifted his arms, and they carried him over to the doctor's office. 'You told me you lost your eye to a Comanche's Bowie knife in single combat, Mr Cannibal,' the young Ranger said as they hefted Wolf through the door. He had a well-bred Louisiana drawl. 'Which was it really, Mr Sommers?'

'An Arkansas toothpick, and an El Paso bar-girl, far as I know, Nolan.'

'That's what I told *you*, Nate. Really,

I've still got the eye, but I wear the patch to make me look less girlish.'

'You,' said Nate Sommers to the doctor. 'You work on him like he was close kin.'

'Look at his nose.' The young Ranger's lip was curled in distaste.

'Yeah, I seen that done before,' the fat man said.

'If this were my friend. I should hold myself ashamed to come off unscathed while he took such a licking.'

'The sheriff held a gun on me,' Tillet said.

'I don't like the look of this sheriff,' the fat man said. 'Being as I'm bald I take all that hair personal. We should do something about him, Nate.'

'Day Hanly's our priority.' Nate Sommers studied Tillet. 'You look as though that name means something to you. You know him?'

'I used to. Why do you want him?'

'He robbed a bank in Longview. Him and his gang.'

'His gang? It can't be the same

86

person.' It didn't seem possible that Day could have got a gang together in such a short space of time.

'Well, Day Hanly is his name and Day ain't like Billy-Bob. It used to be the Harper gang, but Dave Harper got himself shot. Hanly and a man called Mick Murdoch picked the back room of the York and Morely Bank to shoot it out for who bossed the outfit. Murdoch made his peace with a parson and got talkative at the end. So we know the name of the man who shot him.'

'I can't believe Day's killed a man.'

'Well, who knows what'll happen to a man once he starts to go bad?'

'Yeah.' The fat man leered at Tillet. 'Men have done stranger things than that. How do you think I got the name Cannibal?'

8

All the farmers met at Karl's that night and crowded shoulder to shoulder round two joined tables. The Rangers were with them.

'That is why they are all birds of the same feather in that town,' said Willie. 'Because when anyone different to them, anyone decent, comes along they soon show them they are not welcome. And that is what is happening to us.'

'I say we pull down the church and build it somewhere else — somewhere far from Lodestar,' said Gunter.

'The bishop said the church was to be built in Lodestar,' pointed out Father Slattery.

'I also say let us forget about the town. All we need is our church and a store. Let us build them out here.'

'No,' said Karl. 'We need the town.

It has a telegraph, a post office and a stage depot; and when the railroad comes, in Lodestar it will also stop. We need all those things, and we need the protection of the law.'

'Yes, we get very fine protection from the sheriff of Lodestar.'

'That is why we must put our case to the governor of the county.'

'I wish you boys luck,' said Cannibal Beal. 'Governor Andrews is a died-in-the-wool Texan. He ain't got no love of foreigners, and if you ain't Presby, you best be Baptist.'

'He's a bigot then?'

'Hell, no. He's a good boy. He rode with Terry's Rangers in the war. He just draws the line too close. Now me — anybody who is white and who ain't Yankee, I'll call him brother.'

'That's mighty big of you,' said Father Slattery drily.

'Well, the way I see it, you folk have got the makings of Texans in you. So what, if you was born foreign.'

'We were born German,' said Peter,

a reserved man, whose thin face with its large eyes was now showing signs of anger. 'As were Beethoven and Handel.'

'Sure, but that wasn't your fault.'

'Mr Cannibal has a diplomatic touch,' Nolan observed.

'Put a rein on it, Beal,' said Nate Sommers. 'These people invited us to sit at their table and they done us proud — '

'God damn! I'm just a plain-speakin' man. If folk prefer a greasy, finger-kissin' — '

Nate Sommers raised his voice. 'Now, as far as I'm concerned there's only one law in Texas and that's for everybody. It sounds like you folks ain't getting a fair shake from it. But there is quite a bunch of you and every adult male has got a vote to cast. They're holding elections for sheriff in Longview this month, and you're entitled to call one here too. The chief attorney is presiding.'

'There are more of us than there

are of them, I believe,' Karl said thoughtfully.

'But who would we elect?'

'Well, I might be able to help on that,' said Nate Sommers. 'I got a cousin — Frank Holmes his name is — he's twenty years a Ranger, but can't ride long distance any more because of a bad back. He's looking to join the regular police force but hasn't found the right opening yet. You nominate him, and I'll stand guarantee that he's as capable and as honest as they come.'

As the beer flowed, the talk began to turn to less serious matters. Karl produced a violin and accompanied Willie Kellerman's pretty young wife, Greta, in a lilting German air. As Tillet, sitting with Cannibal Beal and Father Slattery, listened to the Ranger tell how he came by his curious nickname, his eyes were often drawn to the corner where Anna sat between Nolan and Heinrich Fischer.

'On the fifth day we ran out of grub,'

Beal was saying. 'We was smack in the middle of the Big Bend and there wasn't no difference to going back or forward — I'd rather die of thirst, hunger draws out. It wasn't till a week later, and not a solitary bone to gnaw, that we caught up with Jake and Montan. They'd got themselves a mule loaded with provisions, canned and dry, and were cooking up a stew when we jumped them . . . '

Anna glanced up and caught Tillet's eye as Nolan and Heinrich chattered into each ear. Tillet dropped his gaze.

'Montan chucked down his gun and up with his hands, but Jake, he was an old-fashioned hardcase and he jumps up to fight. My partner, Joe-Bob, put a bullet in him, and when he quit squirmin' he was dead as a door-knob . . . '

Karl had struck up 'Red River' in waltz-time and now Nolan was holding out his hand, inviting Anna to dance. Heinrich glared at him and Nolan flushed, realizing his mistake.

'Of course, we fell right on that grub. Joe-Bob, he got the pot in his hand and the spoon kinda freezes in mid-swoop and he gives a howl and cusses like a madman. I look, and sure enough, old Jake had gone and squirted a big splash of blood right into that pot. 'Hell', I says to Joe-Bob, pryin' the pot out of his fingers, and the spoon too, 'they say you can put anything in a Mulligan stew'. And, boys, I just stirred that blood in and commenced to feed.'

Heinrich had won Anna's ear again and was speaking rapidly into it. Tillet knew Anna was glancing at him, but he pretended not to notice. He saw the disappointed look the priest gave him, as well. He felt resentment. He supposed there was a reason for everybody doing whatever job they did, and he guessed the priest was just an old busy-body when all was said and done.

'Well, now . . . they say silence is golden, but I never knew a woman who didn't appreciate a silver tongue. If I were you I wouldn't let those two do all the sweet-talking.'

'I ain't much good with fancy words.'

'And plain ones would do just as well. It depends who speaks the words, after all. And if you don't know Anna is waiting for you to speak to her — '

'Look, Father.' Tillet glanced round and said in a low voice, 'It's easy for those two to sweet-talk her. They can look her in the eye without remembering they was the one who crippled her.' Tillet stood and made his way, head down, through the crowd to the door.

As he took his hat from the peg, he turned round and looked over towards Anna. But now she had decided it was her turn to avoid his eye. Everyone was laughing and chattering. They had forgotten that Wolf's being beaten almost to death was the thing that had brought them here and now were taking the rare opportunity of an evening all together to make a party.

Tillet closed the door. After a few steps the sounds of merrymaking became muted, swallowed up in the vast Texas sky.

He had an urge to flee and hide himself. Except that — the brilliant, star-filled sky had never looked so lonely before. But even out here, the music and laughter grated on him unbearably.

They should've left me to swing on that tree, he thought. I'm broke in my spirit. If that wasn't enough, I got to carry the burden of knowing Anna's crippled because of me. That old boy up above sure got it in for John Tillet. I guess You didn't give me one decent chance in my whole life, did You?

In the darkness of the barn he found his saddle by touch. He paused as he was about to lift it off its hook. It was the work of a dog to run out like this without so much as a word. He admired these folk. They were decent and respectable. His mouth hardened and he swung down the saddle.

Maybe too damn respectable, he thought. My ma was a Bible-thumper, but she'd thought nothing of straddling her legs and pissing beneath her skirt on the side of the road. Maybe he came of just too rough a stock for these respectable folk.

As he began leading out his horse, he saw the outline of a figure in the opening of the barn. He recognized the silver halo of hair.

The priest came and grabbed his arm. 'Where are you going?' Tillet could smell the drink on his breath. 'John, this is your chance, your chance for salvation. You might think that you're young, that you'll get other chances — '

'Ain't no need to make a sermon out of it, Father. I don't even belong to your church. I been feeling low lately, but I just need a change. Ain't no big thing.'

'A man's immortal soul is a damned big thing, and I tell you that an angel and a devil are fighting over yours.'

Tillet laughed. 'Are you my angel? I don't see no wings.'

Tillet put his foot in the stirrup, but the priest grabbed his shoulder and shouted in his face, 'You're going to slink off like a dog, feeling sorry for yourself. By God, I could — '

The priest shook his big fist in his face and Tillet gave a shove that sent him staggering back into the shadows beyond the pale stream of light that came through the open door.

Tillet peered into the gloom. 'You all right?'

There was a groan. He went over and found the priest holding his head.

'You all right?' Tillet repeated.

'Don't trouble yourself.'

'Look here, Father, I'm sorry. I know you mean well.' Tillet took his arm. 'Here. Can you stand up?'

The priest got unsteadily to his feet and made for the ladder up to the loft. Whether it was the drink or that he'd taken a crack on the head, he seemed very unsteady now.

'Watch out.'

'I be a'right.'

The priest's foot slipped off the ladder again and he dropped to the rung below. Tillet started up after him. He guided the priest's feet into the rungs.

'Sure, you might as well have a lie-down now and start out in daylight,' the priest said, when they reached the loft. And Tillet discovered that the compulsion to flee had left him.

'I sure am tired,' he said.

'Yes, you lay down and sleep. A man needs a little rest.'

'Yeah, you're right . . . a man does . . . ' Tillet dragged off his boots and sank down on his blankets.

In the night, Tillet began to make sounds in his throat. His arms strained, trying to obey his will and a hand at last managed to reach and fumble at his neck.

The priest lay and watched him strain and twitch. The night seemed to be alive with devils. One, familiar to him, crept up and whispered in his ear. Why don't you wake him and give him a sermon? That's your job, isn't it? Give him the one that's in your heart, Man of Lies. And the Lord said, Let dog eat dog. World without end.

9

'They say you are leaving us,' Anna said conversationally as she laid her basket down on the trestle. 'When do you go?'

Tillet brushed the sawdust off his pants. 'Well, I promised the Father I'd help him put up the rafters, seeing as it's a two-man job and everyone is busy with the harvest.'

'What delights have you brought for us — apart from yourself?' Father Slattery said as he swung a timber off his shoulder and laid it on the trestles.

Anna lifted a pie out of the basket and the priest rubbed his hands and gave an 'Ahh' of appreciation.

'Of course, there's enough work here to keep our John busy till next harvest, what with these plans to build a store as well. You Germans — you're not as quick to rouse as some races, but when you are — look out! I think this town is going to see some changes.' The priest took a mouthful of pie. 'Wonderful, wonderful, wonderful. And you baked this yourself?'

'It is from canned plums. A plums pie.'

'So you see, we must be very nice to John, so that he'll stay with us, for he's worth two donkeys.'

'It is for him to decide what he wants to do.'

'I reckon that's right,' said Tillet.

'Ah, now, how could he leave a place where he is fed as well as this? He'll be a happy man that gets you for a wife.'

'I hope he will be happy.' Anna was acting very pert and carefree today. Tillet had never seen her like this before.

'How could he not be?' cried the priest with a theatrical beetling of his brows.

'Heinrich has asked me to marry

him. I hope to make him happy.'

'Oh . . . ' The priest's frown became genuine. 'Congratulations,' he muttered and continued eating, but with less relish than before.

'Congratulations,' said Tillet.

Anna's smile tensed and a gleam of displeasure flickered in her eyes.

Tillet ground at his pie like a mule on its fodder. He took a morose satisfaction in his show of indifference. Well, that was one less thing to keep him here, he thought.

'Karl and the rest aren't coming into town, are they?' the priest said, shading his eyes and looking to the south. A faint sound of horses could be heard.

The riders emerged out of the brush and, as they approached, Tillet recognized Day Hanly at their head. Dolores rode beside him. He also recognized the lost face of the little half-wit and some others of Dave Harper's gang.

Day stared him in the eye as he approached, and though Tillet could read no hostility in the look, he could detect no definite sign of friendliness either. For a while it seemed they would ride on by, but when they were several yards off Day cried, 'Ho!' and threw up his hand,

Day wore a dark-blue shirt that was stitched with silver. His boots were stiff and new and finely tooled. The mother-of-pearl handles of his pistols stood out sharply against his dark clothes.

'Hi, Cousin.'

'Hi, Day.'

Day's voice was easy. There was no sign of recollection of the night Tillet had seen him humiliated. He was taking satisfaction in the impression he was making, in his new outfit, riding at the head of Dave Harper's men. Tillet found that he was the one who was growing uncomfortable.

'You and the Reverend are mighty busy. What you making?'

'Building a church.'

Day laughed. 'Boy, we sure gone

different ways. You making a church and me raising hell from here to Waco.'

Dolores' voice chimed, faint and fragile. 'Hi, Johnny.'

Now that she had drawn attention to herself she sat with her eyes coyly lowered, permitting herself to be examined. Then she looked up and glanced from Anna to Tillet. She grew thoughtful, then her smile widened again, became mocking. 'I've miss you, Johnny,' she murmured, her eyes glancing at Anna to see her reaction. 'Have you miss me?' Her voice was low and provocative, her eyes hot with meaning.

Someone muttered something in a low, rumbling voice. Day's eyes darkened at the tone of the remark, but he did not look round.

Dolores slid down off her horse and came up to Tillet. She was aware of the sudden tension she had created. Her face was burning with the consciousness of all the eyes on her; at the same time, she was revelling in her own wilfulness.

She exaggerated the swing of her hips as she came closer still.

'Don't you say hello to old friends?'

Tillet was enveloped in her perfume, and now her breast was touching him. It made him think of the touch and smell of an animal when it is young and fragrant — the soft haunch of a kitten.

'Give me a proper greeting. The one you feel in your heart.'

She had forgotten everything, all the eyes upon her, even Tillet, it seemed. Her brown eyes became unfocused and rolled. The blue-tinged whites gleamed before the fine, purplish lids fluttered closed as though she were about to faint. Her hands slid up his chest and then he felt the dry, soft touch of her mouth on his. When she drew away again, her eyes were sharp with triumph.

'Come on, Dolores,' Day barked. 'Let's go.'

She answered in a hard, flat voice 'I tol' you once before — nobody orders me what to do.'

There was another rumbling mutter, and Day's head jerked round. 'You got something to say, McMurtry?'

A big bear of a man, dark and blunt-featured — Tillet had not seen him before — rounded his eyes in mock surprise. 'What?'

The man with the broken nose beside McMurtry was one of Harper's original gang. He had his face lowered and was smothering a smile.

'Well?' Day shouted. It seemed as if he was surprised by the tone of his own voice. He did not wait for a reply, but jabbed sharply with his spurs so that his mount snorted in surprise and began to run on into town.

Laughter rumbled up from McMurtry's belly and shook his beefy shoulders. 'A man who lets a woman get that kind of a grip on him is a pure fool. She'll make him wriggle like a hooked fish.'

The young redhead with the face covered in freckles said, 'I'd like to hear you say that to Day's face. He's already shot a man, remember?'

'How do you know I ain't shot a man?'

The redhead was already riding after Day. As the rest began to kick their horses into movement, the one with the scout's long hair and buck-skins said, 'Are you trying to say you shot your man and you just been hiding your light under a bushel?'

Dolores reached up a hand and fingered Tillet's collar. 'Your shirt is all frayed, Johnny. You ain't growing rich here. How much is he paying you to break your back?'

'It always comes down to how much with your type.' The priest's eyes were hidden. He looked embarrassed and angry. 'You've got the very soul of a whore, Dolores.'

Dolores laughed. 'Nothing.' With her eyes she indicated Anna. 'What's keeping you here — her?'

Tillet shook his head. He felt like a child having words coaxed out of him. The gleam of her eye showed she knew the effect her closeness was having on him, but he could not resent it. 'I guess she's already got herself a fiancé.'

Dolores' brows furrowed slightly. 'Oh, I thought . . . ' She recovered her lazy composure. 'Tha's good. Good for you. She'd just put out any flame you got in you — good little housewife looking for a tame little husband.'

Dolores walked over to her horse. 'Help me, Johnny.' Tillet went over and cupped his hands for her boot. 'We be in town a few days, Johnny. You come see us. We got plans.'

'What a damned mischief-making little devil you are,' said the priest.

'He doesn't like me. Because I'm free. He won't be happy till everyone is chained up like him. Priests . . . You come tonight, Johnny. *Adios.*'

Tillet turned to meet the priest's disapproving stare.

'I don't know why you're looking at me like that,' he said sullenly. 'I ain't even your church.'

The priest said nothing. He jammed the pencil behind his ear and went off to get another timber.

'I'm sick of him pryin' into my business. Who does he think he is?'

Anna had her back turned. She was folding up her napkin and putting it into the basket. She did not answer.

'God damn! I never felt so fenced in and tied up in my life. Not even with my ma.'

'You are finished?' Anna mumbled.

'What?'

'I go back. You are finished?'

'Oh, yeah, thanks.'

Anna began to put the plate with the remainder of the pie in her basket, but her hand was trembling so that the pie slid off the plate on to the timbers.

'Oh — here . . . ' Tillet bent to help her but, as he picked up the pie, it crumbled in his fingers. 'Lord, I'm — are you all right?' Now he could see how her face was flushed with blood and tense with the struggle to control her agitation.

She made a noise as if someone had punched her and winded her. The basket fell and she turned and began to hurry away. Her limp made her roll awkwardly from side to side.

Tillet followed her round the corner of the church. She kept running until she came to a big oak and disappeared behind its bole. He found her sitting on one of its roots wiping tears from her eyes. He put a hand on her arm.

'Oh!' she protested — it was an angry, throaty sound — and pushed his hand away.

Tillet felt lumpish. Resentment built in him and he wanted to say something about female foolishness. But something told him this moment was important and no time to pretend to be stupid. 'Are you going to marry Heinrich?'

'I have a limp. I cannot turn down proposals.'

'Those riders who forced your wagon off the track — I was with them.'

She looked up at him in genuine bewilderment. 'With them? What were you doing with them?'

'I was rustling horses. I'm responsible for your limp.'

'No . . . ' Her lips hung open and she gazed with puzzled eyes into the distance.

'So, if you like, I'll get on my horse right now and not stop till I'm clean out of the country.'

'No. It was not your fault.'

Tillet felt as if he were about to jump off a high rock. 'Then I'm asking you not to marry Heinrich.'

He gathered his courage, reached out his hand and laid it on her shoulder. Where Dolores was light and fragile to the touch, there was a suggestion of heaviness to Anna.

The shadows of the leaves rippled over her lowered head and the big oak seemed to heave low sighs as the breeze passed through it. The priest had begun to saw again. The strokes sounded distant, lost under the dome of the sky.

Anna looked up at him and smiled and Tillet felt he had done something momentous. She rose and began to walk back and Tillet followed along behind her.

As they neared the corner of the church, Tillet became aware of the voice of the sheriff.

'Where do you get the gall — a bunch of foreigners — coming in here and trying to take over this town?'

The priest measured out his words carefully. 'First of all, we are not foreigners; we are American citizens. We are entitled to the protection of the law of the country and we are entitled to vote for whoever we want to represent that law. Now — '

The sheriff cut him short. 'If you think Texas boys will set quiet while a sly-tongued Irisher and a bunch of beer-guzzling, melodeon-playing, square-headed, pop-eyed, God-damned Fritzes take their town off them . . . then you got another think coming.'

10

A harvest moon rode the scudding clouds and its illumination was enough to make the street partly visible through the lamp-lit reflection in Caldwell's window. The tailor, collecting bottles from the sill, screened out the image of the bar-room with the shadow of his hand and tried to get a clearer look at the dark figure he had glimpsed against the façade of the disused assay office. There was not a soul in the street.

'Seeing ghosts,' he muttered. He glanced sharply at a bottle and held it up to the light. There was an inch of beer in it. 'Waste not, want not.' He downed it at a gulp. 'Damned if I don't still want, though.' He tittered and made his way to the bar. ''Scuse me, gents. 'Scuse me,' he chirped cockily, his eyes darting fearfully on all sides to catch the reaction.

'I may have put a bullet in Murdoch, but I respect him,' Day Hanly said. 'He died fighting back. That's how I want to die. With a gun in my hand — spittin' lead.'

'Yeah, I don't hanker to die old, blind and dribblin',' said Pollock, the man in buckskins.

'How do you want to die?' McMurtry prodded his gun against the tailor's spine. 'Headshot or gutshot?'

The tailor knocked over one of the bottles he was laying on the bar. The bartender with the drink-reddened face caught it as it dropped off the edge.

'Mister,' — the tailor rolled his muddy eye towards Day and looked abject — 'could you tell your friend please stop. I got what they call a nervous temp'ment.'

Day was watching Dolores as she walked down the stairs. The conviviality had left his face. Dolores made her lazy way to the table in the corner and sat down.

'Day, is it true?' The little half-wit

pulled Day's sleeve.

'What?'

'Is it true they's got a city made of gold in the jungle down in Mexico?'

'Venezuela. You want to help me find it, Weevil?'

'Match a man to a job,' said McMurtry. 'A fool for a fool's errand.'

'Weevil may not have brain enough for one man, but he's got heart enough for two,' Day said. He was watching Marty, who had come into the saloon and was making his way to Dolores' table.

Marty sat down and began talking to Dolores. He wore his tight, confident smile. Dolores kept her eyes downcast and her face expressionless; her air of languor had deserted her.

'Set up another bottle,' Day told the bartender. He took the bottle they'd been drinking from off the bar and went over to the table.

'Day! Sit down. Play a hand with me.' Marty's tone was friendly, but his expression was a shade too cool and self-confident. The irony of his manner was understated, though. Day looked unsure whether to react or not. He sat down and picked up the cards that were flipped at him.

'Caldwell says he might be able to sell the bunch of papers you picked up back to the bank — they'll want the deeds at least. He'll sound them out through a third party. For the jewellery he'll get you three hundred bucks.'

'Three hundred!'

'I'm telling you what he said, Day.'

The red-haired cowboy with the freckled face carried over his beer and took a chair. He looked very youthful because of the freckles and habitually wore a scowl to offset a naturally open and good-natured face. He cast a wary, unfriendly glance at Marty. Marty made him nervous; but it was partly his own sense of this that led him to sit at the same table as him. 'I don't know why you let that McMurtry join up with us, Day. He's a troublemaker.'

'I can handle McMurtry,' Day said.

He threw down his two pairs and Marty showed him his three eights. Day scowled at Marty's self-satisfied grin. Day's eyes were tired and bloodshot. He'd been drinking steadily since noon.

As Marty dealt again he looked at Dolores and said, 'Shame about Dave Harper.'

'Yes,' Dolores said. She treated Marty with the same wariness as the rest of them.

Marty seemed to thrive on the uneasiness he caused. 'There was another guy, Virge Harbinson. You used to be his woman didn't you?'

Dolores gave him a cold look. 'No.'

'Oh, I thought you were. He came to a bad end too. Somebody cleaned him like a fish — so I heard. Opened him up and cleaned him out. What do you think of that? Must have had it in for him bad, huh?'

Dolores' voice hardened, her accent thickening. 'I said I don' know heem.'

'Jacks and treys.'

'God damn!' Day threw down his hand.

Dolores smiled. 'You know you gotta keep a cool head for poker. You as easy to read as a little boy.' She reached out to brush a strand of Day's hair off his forehead. Day batted her hand away angrily. Her eyes flashed, but Day was not looking at her. 'Deal,' he said.

'Gimme a drink of you' beer, Abilene.'

Dolores reached out and rested her fingers on Abilene's freckled hand. Her fingers brushed slowly up his hand and gripped the bottle-neck. She lifted the bottle out of his hand and tipped it to her mouth, looking at him out of the corner of her eye as she swallowed.

'You a good-looking boy, Abilene. You gotta girl somewhere?'

Abilene did not reply at once but, as Dolores continued staring at him finally he said, 'Ain't got no special girl.'

'That's a shame. Good-looking boy like you . . . with you' beeg, broad shoulders.' Dolores ran her hand slowly over the bulge of his shoulder.

'Listen, Miss Dolores. Day's my friend.'

Day stood up and kicked back his chair. 'Hell, you can have her, Abilene. She ain't nothing but a whore and I'm finished with her.' He threw down his hand and strode over to the bar.

A sharp-featured blonde stood at the end of the bar talking to Torrence. Day spoke to them. Torrence shrugged his shoulders and the blonde gave a shrill laugh then followed Day towards the stairs.

Marty turned Day's cards over. 'He would've took that hand, as well. You play poker, lover-boy?'

Marty's tone was pleasant and Abilene told himself there was no insult to react to. But as he spoke he suspected he was lying to himself. 'I ain't so good at it.'

Marty stood up. 'You hear that, Dolores?' he said as he pocketed his money. 'He ain't so good at it.' He gave Dolores a level stare, but Dolores' eyes were lowered to the table. 'I'll see you later, beautiful,' he said. She shot him a quick, resentful glance, but said nothing. Abilene, feeling he had to react now or be humiliated, began to get to his feet, but he was afraid, and a shake of Dolores' head and a touch of her hand on his arm was enough to stop him.

Dolores followed Marty's back with cold eyes, then she recovered her composure, gave a lazy smile and, picking up the bottle, poured whiskey into Day's glass

'Have a real drink,' she said.

She leaned across the table and held the glass to his lips. He tried to take the glass himself, but she avoided his hand and held the glass to his lips again. He could see down the bodice of her dress.

'Drink.'

He sipped resentfully at the whiskey.

'Come over and sit by me.'

With the same reluctant expression, Abilene went over and sat in Day's chair.

'You wan' kiss me?'

'God damn, Dolores! You know how in hell I do, but not here.'

'If a man wants something bad, he should take it when he wants and where he wants.'

Abilene grabbed her and jammed his mouth against hers, staring defiantly out into the room as he did so. No one was watching.

He had never known a woman could feel like this. He became aware that he was gripping her arm hard and released the pressure, began instead to pat her arm gently with awkward fingers. He would never do a thing in the world to hurt her.

Abilene, still with his arms around Dolores, glanced up guiltily again. At that moment a stranger entered and stopped inside the saloon doorway

He was an unusual figure: long, thin — he had something of the look of a preacher with his black dress relieved by just a small V of white shirt-front. His face was gaunt and hollow, sickly, of a pure-bred Spanish cast. The only other person who had seen him enter was the little tailor who was running a rag over the tables near the door. He stood with the rag in his hand, his mouth pulled open slightly, gazing at the stranger with a mixture of fascination and distaste.

The stranger's head turned and his eyes met Abilene's. The malignancy of the eyes fixed on his jarred him like a sudden slap on the face. In the glitter of them in their darkened sockets, there was something wild and driven. They were the eyes that a man wrought to the limit, facing some extreme experience might have.

When the stranger removed his stare it was as though he had been released from some influence and, as he walked out the door Abilene dismissed him as just some unfortunate whose brain had been turned — sick in the head.

'See? It feel good to take what you want, no? Just know what you want and then take it. What you want, Abilene?'

Abilene's defences were down. His face was as open as a faithful hound's. 'I . . . the only thing I want . . . I just want to make you happy . . . I guess I — I want to marry you.'

Dolores' eyes wrinkled in a smile that was both weary and affectionate. 'You a good boy.'

The little tailor came and began running his grey, evil-smelling rag over the table.

'You see that stranger?'

Abilene gave him an impatient look, but the tailor was too abstracted to notice. His crusted lips hung open and his nose was wrinkled as if he'd smelled something bad. 'Looked like some kind of Spanish don, didn't he? He got killer's eyes if ever I seen them.'

'You ever see a killer's eyes?' Abilene said flatly.

'He was wrong. That's all I know.'

'He rattled you, friend.'

'Yeah, he rattled me. Feel like a worm just come through my winding cloth.' The tailor shuddered. 'Let me have a drink of that whisky, friend.'

The tailor did not notice the blonde approaching. When she tapped him on the shoulder he jumped and the rheum glittered in his flickering eyeballs.

'Harvey, take a bottle upstairs — the gen'lman's in the mood for drinking.'

The tailor hurried off obediently and the blonde sat down beside Dolores. 'That's all he's in the mood for. If ever a man had it bad, it's him. He's like a dog that don't know whether to bark or howl.' The blonde sighed. Her whore's eyes looked back into the past and grew watery. 'Ah, I 'member the time I had them at my feet like you, dearie. You'll not believe it to look at me now — ' She stopped and her eyes sharpened. 'You all right, dearie? You look like you seen a ghost.'

Dolores got to her feet and made for the stairs. There was no trace of her usual indolent saunter. As she hurried blindly down the corridor, a hand grabbed her arm.

'Running back to Day?' Marty said.

Dolores stood passively, not looking at him, waiting to be released. Marty's eyes narrowed as they studied her face. Then his lip curled into a grin. 'I smell fear. A woman of mine don't need to fear nothing — except me, maybe. Day ain't tough enough. Sure, he killed a man, but that don't mean nothing. It's just a question of opportunity.' Marty pulled her close and put his nose against hers. 'I know you, *chacha* — to the core. We were made for each other.'

Dolores tried to pull away, but Marty held her arm fast. 'Remember — when you're ready, I'm waiting.'

When he released her she remained standing as if her will had deserted her. Then she turned and fled down the corridor. Marty grinned.

Day was propped up against the brass bars of the bed nursing the whiskey bottle in his lap. He kept his eyes fixed on the bottle while she approached the bed. She came submissively with her hands clasped beneath her breasts.

'I want to tell you to get out but, God help me, I can't.'

She sat on the bed and spoke in a small, lost voice. 'You the only one for me.'

With a convulsive movement he pulled her to him. He crushed her until a gasp made him realize he was hurting her. He relaxed the pressure but kept holding her. After a while he opened his eyes and studied her, a look of concern on his face.

'What's wrong?'

She began plucking with nervous fingers at his shirt-front. 'Day, take me away from here — far away — please.'

'Sure, honey, sure. If you've got the notion to move. We got business with Caldwell. When that's through, we'll go down on the Gulf, maybe . . . see if we can't spend some of our cash, hey?'

'Day, please. Now. Tonight. I beg of you — you don' — '

He patted her back and said soothingly, 'You're all worked up, angel. Couple of days won't matter, now. You'll see.'

Dolores burst into tears. She tried to speak, but the words that came through were all in Spanish. She babbled the names of God and the Devil, and wailed, '*Estoy en peligro.*'

'What danger?' But he couldn't get any sense out of her. All he could do was hold her helplessly while she suffered like a child in the throes of some agony that only a child can comprehend.

* * *

It seemed inevitable to Abilene. It was like coming out of a dream — the kind you try to will yourself back into while reality prods and pokes and won't let you be until you have to wake up. She'd had a tiff with Day, but when she found out how he really felt about her she'd gone running back without a second thought. That was all.

Abilene finished his beer. When he

got to his feet to fetch another, he felt the pressure of the ones he'd already put away, and headed out the back door instead.

He made his way along the path beaten through the tangled grass to the drainage ditch and unbuttoned his pants.

In the saloon he could hear Pollock's light tenor reaching for a high note. A bray of laughter drowned him momentarily. Up above, the clouds streamed past the moon. Below, the air was still.

God, but she'd felt wonderful. Oh, well, at least a man could get drunk. Hip hurrah for the drink. It went in one end and out the other and eased the heart on the way through. Abilene looked up at the moon and sighed while the grass that overgrew the ditch rustled under the stream of urine.

The moon began to trouble him — for no reason he could see. It had turned into a mad eye glaring down at him. He felt stupid to be spooked like this, out of the blue. But he couldn't help it. He wanted to finish his business and get back inside.

He felt a hand clamp over his mouth, the fingers and thumb digging into his neck behind the jaw, and somebody was working at his throat like a butcher cutting a steak.

Then the hand was gone from his mouth. He knew someone had slit his throat and he began to yell for help. He heard a whistling sound. He raised his hands and felt a little spray of blood spurt over them. Urine began to soak his pants. He tried to call again, but all that came was another whistle. His wind wasn't getting through to his voice box. He had to get inside. He began to turn, but he was pushed forward. His foot went through the grass and met nothing and he fell into the ditch. He pushed himself off the slime of the bottom. The grass had closed over his head again and it was pitch black. He reached up and could just touch the edge. He grabbed handfuls of the grass and tried to climb up, but his arms and legs were like rubber.

11

The crowd that filled Caldwell's saloon on the day appointed for the election of sheriff divided itself into two groups. All the boisterous talk and laughter came from the men who pressed against the bar. The German farmers who had bunched themselves against the wall wore serious faces and their talk was low and private.

Gunter Stitt clicked his watch shut and said, 'Ten minutes to two.'

'They will come.' Karl sat hunched over the table looking straight ahead at the boarded-up façade across the street. 'Willie has never been late for anything in his life.'

'I have made a count,' said Gerhardt. 'If they do not come, then the others will be more than us.' He gazed mournfully at Karl.

'I tell you they will come.'

But at two o'clock neither the brothers Rudolph and Martin nor Willie Haufe had appeared, and Attorney Prescott rose from the table where he had been chatting cordially with Luke Caldwell and began to make his way into the back room to start taking the ballot.

The priest stood up. 'I am going to talk to him. I'll ask him to give us more time.' He caught up with the attorney as he was going through the door of the back room. The farmers watched as the priest stood humbly, with hands clasped at his breast and his neck drawn into his hefty shoulders, while the attorney faced him with a hand on his hip and the other smoothing his flowing moustache. They saw the attorney smile as he replied, but the geniality that had been in his eyes when he'd chatted to Caldwell had faded a little.

'He said if the date and time of the election has been properly posted, then it is not in his power to change either,' the priest told them when he returned. 'He also asks you to vote Zach Prescott for governor of the county.'

While the priest was pleading with the attorney, Tillet had noticed Marty staring over at Wolf. Wolf was aware of it too. He began to twitch and the scabbed-over scars stood out against the whiteness of his face. Finally he said in a breathy voice that this was supposed to be a place to drink and he was going to buy a beer, but some of the farmers knew that he was nervous and ashamed of it, and they were afraid that he was going to do something reckless. The priest got on his feet again.

'And that's a good idea. But sit where you are and I will buy for all of us. Come you with me, John, will you?'

As Tillet stood at the bar, the blacksmith rasped with a thumbnail at his sideburn over the beers the bartender was setting out on the counter. With a tired little smile and a sly glimmer in his eye he said, 'That your job — fetch for them?'

The farmers lined up at the door of the back room after everyone else had voted. When the last of them had cast their ballot, there was still no sign of Rudolph, Martin or Willie, and the attorney came out and announced that the office of Sheriff of Lodestar and those environs specified in the County Survey Office of Longview would continue to be held by Sheriff Griffiths.

Griffiths' supporters roared and made the boards shake with their stamping. As the sheriff stood having his back slapped and his hand pumped he bared his square white teeth in a bulldog grin at the farmers.

It was this, it seemed, that finally made Karl lose his restraint. Aiming his finger at Caldwell, he shouted, 'Do you know that this man owns this town — and also the sheriff?' The attorney stopped in his round of handshaking and cast an embarrassed look from

Karl to Caldwell. 'Do you know that here outlaws are free to go about as they please?'

The sheriff's grin turned down at the corners and he stuck out his square chin. 'You might be able to slander people in your country, mister, but we got a law against it here.'

The attorney looked at his watch. 'Gentlemen, I — '

'Mr Prescott.' Caldwell took the attorney by the sleeve and the attorney turned to him gratefully. 'I meant to ask — you know Simon Trimmer? Of the Trimmer Logging Company? The thing is, he happens to be a good friend of mine, Simon.'

'Is he? You don't say.' The attorney beamed at Caldwell as Caldwell walked him in the direction of the door.

'Now, the next time I speak to Simon, you can be sure that I'm going to mention those sound plans of yours — just as you explained them to me today.'

'Well now . . . '

As Caldwell was ushering the attorney through the door, Karl called after him, 'New world — old ways.'

Caldwell and the attorney gave him a look that seemed to suggest he had embarrassed himself in public. The priest laid a hand on Karl's shoulder and sighed, 'Patience, old friend, patience. There is nothing we can do here. Let's leave.'

Karl rounded on the priest. 'That too is the old way. Be patient. Trust God. We will all be happy in Heaven.' Karl's disdain was all the more telling by contrast with his usual gentleness, and the priest's face darkened under it.

When Wolf said, 'Let us finish our beer and pay for it like honest Texans — for that is what we are supposed to be', Karl and the rest agreed. They did not want to stay, but they were not in the mood for bolting like frightened rabbits either.

Tillet had a foreboding. He whispered to the priest, 'We're sure asking for trouble staying here.' But the priest shrugged his shoulders morosely.

Tillet sat down. As he raised his glass, he caught sight of Dolores swaying down the stairs. There was an exaggerated laziness to her step. Her eyelids drooped heavily and her face was blank and puffed. Marty grabbed her arm as she sauntered past and she allowed herself to be drawn limply to him. Marty spoke to her with a tight, hard smile on his face while she cast a sleepy glance around the room.

Her eyes lit on Tillet and stopped. She shrugged herself free of Marty and approached the table.

'You come to see me, Johnny? Shoulda lef' you' friends at home.' Her voice was slurred with drink. 'I'm glad you come when Day's not here. He gets jealous, you know. Poor Day. He's gone on a little job.'

'Just what kind of a little job?' the priest asked her, his voice hard and suspicious.

Dolores looked at him and laughed. 'Stick to your prayers, Padre; the

137

business of this world is not for you.'

She came and stood over Tillet. She was close enough for him to be aware of her perfume and the heat of her body, and he couldn't help return her smile as she stared down boldly into his eyes. When she slipped into his lap and snuggled against him like a kitten he wasn't surprised. She took his beer out of his hand and, while she sipped it, her gaze rested on Marty. Marty returned the look, his hard, self-possessed smile unchanged.

Tillet was aware of the eyes of the farmers on them. For a moment he felt resentment for their stolid, disapproving faces, but he was about to ease her off his lap when the priest made a sound of disgust and grabbed her arm.

'Ach! That's enough of your shenanigans.' He jerked her out of Tillet's lap and flung her away and then seemed to forget about her as if she were a cat he had just kicked out the kitchen door.

Dolores stood in a crouch, her left

hand holding the arm on which a red blotch from the pressure of the priest's fingers could be seen. The priest might have forgotten her, but for Dolores nothing in the world existed but the priest. Her eyes bored into the back of his head and hate seemed to coil in her body.

'You touch me,' she hissed. 'You put you' filthy priest's hands on me. Who you think you are? I know wha' you are; you piece of cess-pit filth. I know what all you priests are. The man who took my virginity was a dirty priest.'

The priest got to his feet and picked up his hat.

An expression of triumph came over Dolores' face. 'You like to make out you are better than everybody else, don't you? Hey, Johnny.' She smiled maliciously. 'Did he tell you that he had me? Uh? He had me in the back of his wagon, with his crucifix roun' his neck.'

The priest, about to push past her, stopped dead. He shouted, 'You dirty, lying, little slut,' and slapped her.

Marty pushed himself off the bar and strode down the room. 'OK, Rev, how are you with somebody your own weight?'

Dolores shrieked, 'I wan' you to kill him.'

'Is that what you want?'

Tillet took the priest's arm. 'Come on, Father. Let's get out of here.'

The priest's face was dark. 'I'm in the mood to fight.'

'Not with him.'

The door of the saloon opened and Day Hanly strolled in followed by four of his men. They paused while they took in the tense atmosphere.

'What's going on?' Day said.

'The Reverend here hit Dolores,' Marty told him. 'Now I'm about to break his face.'

As the priest began taking off his coat, Tillet went up to Day and said quietly, 'You gotta stop it, Day. I seen Marty fight. He's a killer. The priest's an old man. He hasn't got a chance.'

'Ain't nothing I can do. Marty don't take orders from me.'

Karl and some of the farmers were gathered around the priest trying to persuade him to leave, but he was rolling up his sleeves with determination. Tillet was about to go to him when Day put a hand on his shoulder. 'Wait. I still count you as a friend, Johnny. And you know when I call a man a friend he can have my last dollar bill.' He called, 'Marty. Hold on. He hit Dolores. That makes it my fight.'

Day took off his hat and undid his gunbelt saying, 'Well, Reveren', that age-old battle 'twixt virtue and sin gonna go to another round.' He put up his hands. 'When you're ready.'

As soon as the priest raised his guard Day was on him like a mountain cat. The priest covered his face and hunched up and took the punches on his head and shoulders. Then he surged forward, raised his right fist as though it held a hammer and brought it down with a hook at the end of the swing. The punch did not travel far, but it caught Day backing, off balance already, and he went down on one knee.

The priest hadn't seen Day go down. He was still bent over with his face covered. Day rose up, his cheekbone blotched red, his eyes angry. The priest straightened and looked out from behind his guard just as Day ran at him. He fell back before his charge, but Day's skull rammed him in the chest, while his fists swung overhand and underhand, into his face and into his ribs and stomach. The back of the priest's knees caught a chair and the floorboards shook as he hit them. Day dropped on his chest. The priest made a grab for Day's wrists, but Day evaded his hands.

'Give up. I got you beat.'

The priest grabbed Day's thigh with both hands. He took two blows in the face before he heaved Day off him and scrambled to his feet. With his left hand before him like a blind man feeling his way, he stumbled after Day. The men scattered and Day backed into the bar. He stood with his back against the bar and swung his fists.

The priest came on through the blows. The fingers of his left hand twisted up a handful of Day's hair and held his head while his right fist clubbed it. Day sank to his knees and the priest released his grip. Day got to his feet again. His left eye was opened up and filling with blood and the right was unfocused. His legs looked about to go. He came forward on wobbling legs and raised a fist. The priest waited for him and pushed him away

Day blundered back into Dolores, clutched at her, smearing her blouse with blood. Dolores made an angry, panicked sound and pushed him off. Day hit the bar and slid down it till he sat with his legs outstretched, his head rolling on his neck.

Dolores stared down at him. Her head was tossed back and her eyes were wild. With a sudden swirl of skirts, she turned and ran for the stairs.

Day rolled his head back and squinted with his right eye up at the priest. His words came out slurred. 'You wan' try guns?'

Tillet stepped quickly to the side of the priest. 'No, Day.'

'Then get him the hell ou' here.'

Outside, as they bunched around the priest, Tillet could hear triumph in the exchanges in German. Heinrich clapped him on the back and said, 'You taught a good lesson to him.' But the priest pushed Karl's handkerchief away from his face and said, 'I have a misgiving. Rudolph and Martin's farm is the closer, isn't it?'

'I also have a misgiving in my heart,' said Karl. 'Let us go there quickly.'

A savage outburst broke out somewhere behind the saloon.

'*Teufel!* Wolves.' Gerhardt's big scared eyes rolled back in the direction of the growling and squabbling noises.

12

Gunmetal clouds had filled up the sky and darkened the afternoon. A dust-devil capered outside the church.

'Look! Wolf!'

As he gave the priest a hand up on to the wagon, Tillet looked back and saw the lean hindquarters of a coyote disappear into the brush behind the buildings.

'In its mouth it have a hand — the wolf — ' There was a pleading look in Gerhardt's round eyes.

'You are a crazy man.'

They found Rudolph and Martin tied to their bed-heads. Martin, excitable and cranky, broke into a tirade as soon as he saw them. Strangers had come. They thought they'd come to rob them, but they'd taken nothing.

'They wanted to prevent you from voting,' Karl told them. 'It will be the

same for Willie and Greta. Poor Greta
. . . she is so timid. Quickly, we must
go to them.'

They stopped at Karl's house and
picked up Mrs Miller and Anna
— 'Better a woman to comfort a
woman,' the priest said — and hastened
out to Willie's farm.

The dream afternoon was filled with
the baying of dogs. As they took the
rise that led to the sheltered hollow
where the farm lay, they heard another
sound rise above the noise of the dogs.
It was thin and desolate, rising and
falling.

'What is that?'

'In the village where I was born they
would call it a banshee.' The priest
sketched the sign of the cross. 'God
have mercy on poor sinners.'

The massive dark clouds hanging
above them, the distant baying of the
dogs, and that desolate keening all
worked on Tillet's nerves. As they
rolled through the neat bean-rows he
felt a sense of foreboding grow in his

mind as the farmhouse grew steadily before his eyes.

In the closed space of the house, the keening was dreadful to listen to. Karl and the priest hesitated at the door to the kitchen, both white-faced and sick-looking. Then Karl put his hand on the door and pushed it open.

Willie's young wife sat on the floor with her skirts rucked up. There was blood on her thighs. She swayed slightly from side to side. Wisps of her fine hair had stuck to her wet cheeks and her eyes were swollen with crying. But she was not crying now. The keening seemed to come from her without her being aware of it.

Willie was tied to a chair. It was toppled over and he lay with his cheek pressed against a rush mat.

As they raised Willie from the floor, Tillet noticed a kitchen knife stuck in the boards of the wall. He pulled it out and cut Willie free. When Willie tried to speak, tears suddenly flooded his eyes and all he could do was sob while the farmers pressed around him and patted his shoulders.

The women got Greta into a chair, and Mrs Miller stood beside her holding and rocking her. The keening was muffled against her bosom.

Willie began to speak in German.

Tillet laid the knife on the table. A watch with its back off lay on the table. Willie was very good at fixing mechanical things. He was stocky and appeared awkward, but his hands were capable of the most delicate tasks. His manner was a little surly and he seemed to prefer to be busy than to talk, but he was always ready to help and he was well respected among the farmers.

Willie clutched the priest's sleeve and cried out in German. The priest stood with his eyes lowered, a look of pain on his face. Willie said in English, 'How can God allow such things?'

The priest made no reply, but took Willie's hands in his and patted them. In English, Willie continued, his voice hardly more than a whisper, 'She was a virgin . . . she said she could not marry ever . . . she had horror of it. It was only by making her believe I would . . . respect her . . . that I could persuade her to marry me. How else would an angel like her have such as I?'

Karl grasped Willie's shoulder and squeezed it. Willie looked up at the priest accusingly. 'Is this how men are in America? What they did . . . the things . . .'

The priest blessed him and began to pray. Someone started to mutter a prayer in German. One by one the other farmers joined in. Mrs Miller bowed her head and began to pray and Anna followed her example.

Tillet, his head bowed, glanced at Greta. Her eyes, which so far had remained unseeing, moved and fixed on his, making him start. She began to look round at the people and objects in the room as if she had never seen them before. She rose out of the chair, slowly. Mrs Miller laid a hand on her.

At the touch of the hand on her arm she lunged across the table and snatched up the knife.

The two women screamed and sprang to their feet and grabbed her as she stabbed herself. Tillet could see that an inch or more of the blade had gone into her.

They laid her down and ripped open her dress to examine the wound. As they cleaned and bandaged it, she stared up, empty-eyed again, past the faces that leaned over her.

When they'd carried Greta to her bed, the farmers gathered in the front room. They spoke in German. Tillet and the priest found themselves excluded until Karl said, 'Willie speaks of a big man and another with a broken nose. Martin and Rudolph spoke of a man with long hair and another, blond-haired, wearing a shirt with fancy silver stitching on the front of it — '

'Hanly,' said the priest.

Tillet blurted, 'Day couldn't have known about this.'

'You are a friend of this Hanly, it seems to be,' Wolf said.

Willie gave a grunt, angry and questioning. He got to his feet, his big head drawn into his shoulders. '*Vas?*' he said, staring at Tillet, his eyes glittering and hostile.

'Now,' Karl said, making a calming motion.

'He was talking with this Hanly in the saloon,' Wolf said. 'Very friendly they seemed to be.'

'This is true,' someone agreed.

Willie started for Tillet. The priest and Karl grabbed him. But he was strong. He dragged them with him and hit Tillet in the chest with his palm, making him stagger back.

'I'll leave,' said Tillet.

Karl turned to him, his kindly eyes screwed up in distress. 'Just wait outside until we have made things calm, John. I'm sorry.'

Tillet stood on the porch in the darkening afternoon watching a hen and her chicks run this way and that in the dirt in front of the house. After a while, Anna came out. Her face was troubled but her body was calm and still and, as she stood beside him looking out over the bean-rows, he felt the same sense of peace her presence always gave him.

'I guess I should've kept my mouth shut in there.'

'Willie also turned on Father Slattery. He called him an outsider. But it is because he is so . . . so . . .'

'I know.'

'Let us go back inside. They are calmer now.'

'Anna . . .' He turned her to face him, but he kept his eyes lowered. 'I want to ask you . . . I been trying to think things out . . . I want to ask you — will you come away with me? We could go to the coast. I could get a job.'

He waited for an answer. When none came, he looked up. Her eyes were far away and sad.

'I thought you felt the same kind of

way as I feel about you.'

She began to twist her fingers in agitation. 'These are my people. I cannot leave them. I would be like a plant when it is pulled out of the ground.'

'But we could have our own family. You'd soon settle and be happy.'

She was trembling and looked as if she might cry. Despite that, he sensed a firmness in her.

'So that's it?'

She looked at him. 'There is no need for anyone to go. Why do you not come inside now?'

'You go along in. I'll be in soon.'

But still he lingered on the porch while the light seeped away and the hollow lay waiting for darkness to take it. The longer he waited the harder it was to go back in. A lone bird flew across the sky, wheeled and headed south. Day had told him about a Tennessee ploughboy who'd gone south to Mexico and become a general. God didn't stamp farmer on us when

He made us, he'd said.'

When he heard the door open behind him his heart began to beat faster. He thought Anna might have been afraid he would leave and had come back out. But the step was too heavy and it was the priest who came and leaned on the porch-rail beside him. He sighed and rubbed the back of his neck as if he'd just taken a break from a hard day's work.

'The poor girl's wits have gone. Only time will tell if they'll come back to her. They were talking about getting their guns and going into town.'

'Father, I know Day didn't have nothing to do with this — what happened to Mrs Haufe, I mean.'

'Karl and I talked them out of going after them. We're going to get the Rangers.' The priest turned his head slightly and looked at Tillet out of the corner of his eye. 'John, I want you to do it. Go to Longview and bring the Rangers back here. To make it clear whose side you are on.'

'But . . . Day's my friend.'

The priest looked back out over the darkening hollow. 'You're young, John. You have more friendships ahead of you. You'll get something from each. And give something too. You'll learn what you can . . . And when there's nothing more to take or give, nothing left to learn, you'll move on.'

The breeze gusted and rattled the shutters. The priest shivered. 'It's cold. Let's go inside.'

The priest went through and left the door open for him. The lamps were lit inside and he could see Anna setting kindling in the fireplace. Wind moaned down the hollow and gusted coldly against his back. Tillet raised himself from the porch-rail and went inside.

13

Longview was a lumber town. The sawmill on the outskirts whined busily and the air was fragrant with the scent of fresh sap. It was also the head-quarters of one of the six permanent companies of Texas Rangers. Tillet was directed to a building behind the main square and in a bare, white-washed office opposite the stables he found Nate Sommers scratching entries in a ledger.

Sommers, while he used a piece of blotting-paper to remove the nib of his pen, said, 'I guess you know there's a reward for Day Hanly.' He looked up at Tillet speculatively

Tillet felt that a shamed look had come into his face. His voice was low. 'I don't want no reward. All I want is a Ranger's badge.'

'Rangers don't wear badges.' Sommers

chose a new nib from a box on the desk. 'So you want to be a Ranger, huh?'

'Uh-huh.'

As the seconds went by, Tillet felt his head begin to twitch, but he made up his mind he wasn't going to say a word until the Ranger spoke first.

'Day was my friend,' he blurted out. 'I don't aim to turn rat on him then run and hide.' He was nettled that the Ranger had got him gabbling just by sitting fiddling with a pen, but he continued, 'I want to be with you when you take him.'

'Well, fact is, we can use the help. Most of the company is down on the Sabine with D Company out of Tyler. Nolan's out now trying to round up Beal. Soon as they get back we'll start for Lodestar. I guess we can enlist your German friends?'

'You won't have any trouble with that.'

'Good thing you don't want that reward. Somebody's already claimed it.'

Tiller watched while the Ranger fiddled with the pen-nib some more.

'Yes, just this morning. Your friend from Lodestar who tried to pull off the German boy's face. And a Dolores Villegas. They're in town now, waiting to collect. But they won't get the money till we bring Hanly in.'

★ ★ ★

In her dream, Dolores asked her mother to help her up.

'They say you have not been a good girl,' her mother said.

'I am a good girl, Mama,' she told her.

'*Pobrecita*.'

'Mama, give me your hand. Please, Mama.'

She reached for her mother but it was as if her mother's hand was made of smoke. She slipped into a black emptiness. She felt she was falling, like a lump of lead, but there was no wind to ruffle a hair of her head.

Dolores jerked awake from the sickening sensation of falling.

Her hand felt for the lamp. When it was lit, she looked at the clock. Marty would be back any minute. Then, Marty could wait. She would not hurry. But still she got out of bed and began to dress.

The outer door of the suite opened and footsteps crossed the room. The knob on the bedroom door twisted.

Marty's voice came through the panels. 'You locked the door?'

'You don' know who is about. I be just one minute.'

She slipped on her dress and fastened it before the mirror. She liked how the crimson silk brought out the richness of her skin and hair. She was glad she was not blonde like an Anglo, pale and bloodless. But she was glad the Indian did not show in her eyes.

'You gonna be all night in there, angel?'

Marty's hard, dangerous voice sent a little tremor through her. Marty frightened her. But he frightened everyone else too. She liked that. In that way he made her feel safe.

'Be patient,' she said. There was a little shake in her voice. She was glad. She wanted him to hear it. It would please him. Marty would take a lot of working on. Marty was hard, and sharp like a razor

A sudden creak of floorboards came from next door as Marty jumped up and took a few impatient steps. She stifled her nervous urge to hurry and drew the stocking slowly up her thigh. It was all right to let him know he scared her a little, but she would show she had the spirit to resist it.

You had to be careful what you showed. When a man showed her that his heart was in her hands, then a devil made her close her fingers and squeeze. Poor Day. Now he would look like someone had pulled out his insides. Well, that was how it was. You could make a man dance to your tune when you were young and had looks, but when you got old, got fat, started to grow a moustache . . . then your *tortillas* better be good, and you'd better know how to wash and scrub —

'That ain't for me,' Marty said.

There was a clatter, the sound of glass breaking. She could imagine the waiter's nervousness with Marty's killer's eyes on him.

'Fer Chri' sake . . . well, don't just stand there, bones . . .'

Marty said something. She couldn't catch what. But the tone of his voice had changed. There was something more serious than irritation in it.

She heard a muffled scuffling from the other side of the door. That poor waiter. Marty must be bullying him. She ran her hands luxuriously up the taut, cool silk from her hips to her breasts. The poor, frightened little —

A scream made her jump and clutch her neck. *Dios!* What had he done? They did not need trouble. Not here.

She went to the door but, as she

gripped the key to turn it, there was a heavy crash on the door that rattled it on its frame. She jumped back.

There were crashing sounds, heavy thumps on the walls. The lamp on the dresser rattled and the mirror shivered. The thudding and banging noises stopped and there came faint sounds that she could not identify. These stopped too and there was silence.

As quietly as she could, she went down on her knees and put her eye to the keyhole. All she could see was the back of a chair and a small area of striped wallpaper. She kept looking until the draught through the keyhole made her eye fill with water.

He was out there.

She tried to control her breathing in case it could be heard. But soon she found she was almost choking. Covering her mouth and her nose with her hands she rose to her feet. The crack of her knee-joint sounded like a rifle-shot to her. She backed on her toes away from the door and as silently as she could gasped in a lungful of air. She heard a little rattle and realized it was her teeth. She clamped her jaws shut, clutched them with her hands. She was shuddering from head to foot.

He was there. She knew.

Perhaps she could smell him. Fear had sharpened her senses. She could smell everything. She could smell the varnish on the door and a wild, violent stink beyond it.

Footsteps began to cross the floor. She darted to the window and then from the window to the bed, crouched to crawl under it. The outer door opened and closed.

Crouched by the bed, she waited, her eyes fixed on the door, until the whirls of varnished grain became eyes that stared back at her. Then slowly she rose and approached the door.

She was afraid of a trick. But, as she had known he was in there before somehow, in the same way now she knew he was not.

Still she stood there for a long time staring at the door, listening to the slow tick of the clock and its quiet chime as it struck the quarter, before she turned the key and opened the door.

Marty sat on the sofa against the wall. His white shirt-front and his lap and the upholstery of the sofa were soaked in blood. His mouth bulged open and his bleeding tongue was sticking out of it. Not his tongue —

'He eats his *cojones*.'

She turned and already he was through the door. Darkness swept in on her and she could only see a black shape coming. And the eyes . . . Lucifer's pride and rage in them.

Woman, it is your time at last. The words in Spanish throbbed inside her brain.

The touch of his fingers shocked her awake. She flew through the door, banged it shut and turned the key. The latch of the window was coated with paint. She heaved at the sash, moaning.

Casting about, her eyes lit on the Bible on the dresser. She snatched it up and threw. It bounced off the pane of the window and the thought came to her, God has condemned me. At each crash on the door she gave a cry. There was no chair to throw through the window. In her desperation she took hold of the heavy dresser. She managed to stagger back a few steps. The lamp fell and smashed leaving her in darkness.

When the wood of the doorframe began to rip she started to scream. She snatched at a drawer of the dresser, shook it from side to side to try to unstick it, stumbled back with it in her hands and ran to slam it into the window. The glass shattered. She smashed the spears of glass out of the window with the drawer.

As she clambered through, the doorframe splintered and he was in the room. The glass of the window ripped her leg. She squeezed her eyes shut at the drop and let herself go. The roof of the porch quaked when she crashed on to it. She rolled down it, breaking her nails as she tried to clutch on to the end shingles, and hit the back alley feet first.

Above her head the roof boomed and rattled.

She dashed towards the sound of trotting horses, realizing as she ran that she was going away from the main street, heading towards the deserted stalls of the market square.

A team of horses trotted out of a side street.

At the frantic cry she gave, one of the two men on the wagon pulled out a gun. 'What is it? Somebody bothering you?'

She scrambled onto the seat beside them. '*Si. Si.* In the name of Jesus, I beg you to go.'

When they came to a street with a lit-up saloon and one or two people strolling along it, the driver slowed down and asked, 'Where do you want to go! lady — the sheriff?'

'No — I — where are you going?'

'Well, we're making a night run to Dunn's Staging Post — passing through Lodestar.'

'Yes. Lodestar. Take me there. I have friends in Lodestar.'

'Ma'am, you look like you've seen the Devil.'

Dolores looked ahead and whispered, 'The Devil . . . yes, I have seen the Devil.'

'All right, I ain't nosy.' The young man beside Dolores took the blanket off his knee and gave it to her. He gave a shy smile and said, 'Yeah, I guess a woman can raise the Devil in a man.'

14

They heard the barking of a hound and saw a rabbit bound out of the scrub. Under the sky pressing down low and sombre, with no breath of wind to disturb the dead stillness of the air, the blast sounded like a cannon let off in a cavern and the horses threw back their heads in alarm. As the rabbit hopped up the granite slope, the rifle blasted again and dust puffed five feet wide of it.

'Men, look out,' said Cannibal Beal. 'Only thing safe round here is that crittur.'

They caught a glimpse of a blond head in the scrub. The hound ran out and darted, head low, across the level and up the slope after the rabbit. Then a boy appeared lugging a Winchester rifle.

'That's Heinz. Gunter Stitt's boy,' Tillet said.

Nate Sommers reined his horse.

Heinz stood like an illustration of one of the old frontiersmen, standing with their long rifles reaching to their shoulders. His eyes behind their pale lashes had a diffident but unafraid look. They gave him a grown-up air. But his body had the willowy awkwardness of a boy who has recently put on a spurt of growth.

'Is your pa at home, son?'

'Papa's in church. It's Sunday. Everyone's in church.'

'How come you're not?'

'I'm sick.'

Cannibal Beal fixed a fierce eye on the boy. 'You don't look terrible sick.'

A small grin appeared on Heinz's face and his colour deepened slightly.

'How far to town?' Nate Sommers asked.

'Two mile — about,' Tillet said.

Heinz had forgotten his bashfulness and was staring frankly at Cannibal Beal. 'What age do you have to be to join the Texas Rangers?' he asked.

169

'You want to be a Ranger?'

'Yes, I want to. When I grow up.'

'Well, that's fine, son. We need marksmen like you.'

'With a bit of luck, we'll get them all together at church service,' said Nate Sommers.

As they rode through the morning that seemed to grow darker rather than brighter, Tillet heard barking and looked back to see the boy and the dog running after them. They must have taken a short-cut through the scrub and come back out on the trail only a couple of hundred yards behind. Tillet wheeled and rode back.

The boy stood with his rifle cradled on his chest, panting. The dog ran to investigate the dung Tillet's mount had begun to drop.

'Run along home, Heinz,' he told him.

'Are you going after outlaws?'

'I'll tell you about it later. But I want you to go home. Hear, now?'

The boy looked at him from behind

the pale fringes of his lashes, a little resentful, but resigned, and Tillet felt sorry to be just another grown-up giving orders.

The dog followed for a while, but when Tillet looked back down the road the boy was still standing as he'd left him with the gun cradled in his arms.

The farmers' horses, gigs and wagons were tied at the rail running along the side of the church that faced away from the town. As they tethered their own mounts among them, only a solitary cough from inside gave evidence that the church was occupied. The doors were open and Nate Sommers removed his hat and led them through.

With the dullness of the morning it was grey and dim inside. As they walked down the central aisle with the new boards clattering under their feet, Tillet thought he could make out the quiet droning sound of a little girl trying to stifle her crying behind her closed lips. The priest stood silently in the pulpit and watched them coming.

Nate Sommers cleared his throat. He spoke in a normal voice but his words rang out loudly in the gloomy stillness of the church. 'Sorry to bust in on you . . . ' He stopped and stared at the priest. 'Something wrong?'

'Everything's just fine.'

Tillet and Nolan whirled round. The other two Rangers took their time in turning. Day Hanly was standing up in a pew at the back of the church. He had a gun pointed at the head of Peter Schroedel sitting next to him. 'Get them pistols to the floor.'

They looked at Nate Sommers. Peter Schroedel's eyes widened as the barrel was pushed against his temple.

Nate Sommers began to undo his cartridge belt and nodded for the others to do the same.

The big man, the one Tillet had heard called McMurtry, rose up from another pew. Here and there the others got to their feet: the one with the broken nose, the long-haired one, the little half-wit, and there were

172

two brothers, Apache and Mexican half-breeds, that Tillet recognized from the night he'd spent with Dave Harper's gang. He spotted Dolores sitting among the women.

'They knew you were coming,' said the priest.

Nolan, standing beside Tillet, looked at him and said, 'I think we can thank this gentleman for that.'

Tillet shook his head, 'I never — '

'It was this little chilli pepper.' Nate Sommers nodded to where Dolores sat. She had removed the shawl from her head and shaken out the heavy mass of her hair.

'Be careful,' said Day, grinning as he came down the aisle. 'You're talking about the girl I love.' He stopped beside Dolores and leaned across the woman sitting beside her to take her hand and kiss it. He dropped his grin and fixed his eyes on her. 'It's true. You came back to me. Maybe saved my life this morning. And I'd give my life for you, too. I'd give my everlasting soul if I had to.' He straightened. 'I ain't afraid to say it.' He came on down to where the men were gathering around the Rangers in the space between the congregation and the altar. 'Yeah, when I give my heart I give it.' He paused and looked at Tillet. 'And when I give my hand, I put my heart behind it . . . You keep peculiar company, Johnny. What're you doing with the Rangers?'

Tillet kept his eyes on the hat in his hands. 'I reckon I'm a Ranger. I came to arrest you.'

Day's voice became low and hard. 'You know it's hangin' for me? I never figured you for a false friend.'

One of the half-breed brothers came close to Tillet bringing a stale, bar-room smell of tobacco and alcohol, and the stink of spoiled meat caught in the teeth. 'He was with you the day you joined up with Dave. He's supposed to be your frien' and he put the knife in your back.' Tillet saw the slap coming and half batted it off with his hat. The hat hit him in the face instead.

Meanwhile, the other half-breed was standing in front of Nolan, staring with hatred at his well-bred face. He curled back his lip. The protruding white teeth were crusted with black along the gums. 'Rangers! They used to shoot my people on sight down on the Bravo. Murdering scum.' He moved along to Cannibal Beal and said, 'I guess you would've like to hang yourself a couple of Mex's, eh — man with too much belly and not enough eye?'

'I'd've liked nothin' better, greaser.'

The half-breed hawked and drew back his head to spit. Cannibal Beal laid a hand on his face and pushed, and the half-breed staggered back against McMurtry. He snatched out his gun, but McMurtry grabbed the barrel and held it down.

'Let go me, Mac!'

'Hold on.'

'Yeah, everybody cool down.'

The big man looked at Day with

eyelids drooping and his small mouth hanging slack. 'That's right. Cool down and let's do this thing properly.'

Day's eyes sharpened at the tone of McMurtry's voice. 'What're you talking about? Do what?'

'Hang 'em.'

A glimmer appeared in McMurtry's eye at the effect these words produced on Day. Releasing the half-breed, his eyes flickered from him to his brother and what he saw in their faces excited him. 'This ain't no Robin Hood and his merry men outfit, is it?' His voice was hard and sure now. 'I say serve them like they'd serve us.' He had turned away from Day and was speaking to the others. 'There's nothing walks or crawls that's lower than a lawman. At least we know which side the law we're on. The half of them are bigger thieves than us, but they'd still stand and watch us twitch on a rope, huh? Damned hypocrite lawmen. Well now it's our turn, men, we'll serve them like they serve us.'

'Forget it, McMurtry,' Day said. 'It ain't my style. Killing in a hot fight is one thing, but I won't kill a man cold. Now, everybody's just gonna stay here in the church till our friend arrives this afternoon. Then we sell our merchandise and disappear.'

McMurtry turned round. 'I thought nobody laid down the law in this outfit. Or don't the merry men get to have their say,' McMurtry grinned.

Day's eyes flashed with anger, but he spoke quietly and slowly. 'I ain't laying down the law, McMurtry: you're out on your own.'

'Well why don't we put it to the vote? What do you say, Paco?'

'Me?' The half-breed had a hungry, reckless expression on his face. 'What do I say?' He stuck out his tongue and crossed his eyes, pulling at an imaginary rope above his head. 'I say hang 'em!'

McMurtry nodded. 'You said the right thing — Dan?'

The broken-nosed man sucked his

teeth with an air of consideration, then looked up. 'Let 'em dance.' He let his gaze travel coldly over the Rangers, one by one. His eye flickered when it met Nate Sommers'.

'Ramon?'

The priest shouted in a voice of wrath, 'You are standing before God's altar!'

The grin dropped suddenly from the second half-breed's face. He glanced with round eyes at the crucifix, whose new flesh-coloured paint made a pale glow in the shadows behind the altar. His brother, with a jerk of his head, sent a jet of spittle that hit the silver chalice and screamed, 'That for your altar! You no-good dirty priests! You are all hypocrites and whore-masters. How would you like we hang you too, eh? The Devil has a place for you and your kind. Priests swarm like maggots in the cesspit of Hell.' He ran over and grabbed his brother by the shirt-front, began shaking him. 'Ramon says let them dance.'

His brother, the grin back on his face, batted away the hands shaking him.

McMurtry's voice was swollen with his sense of power. It rolled through the church. 'Pollock?'

The long-haired man said, 'I don't know, Mac.'

McMurtry put on a whiny voice. 'I don't know, Mac. Jesus Christ, Pollock. You say that? Didn't they hang your own pappy? Didn't you tell us how Sheriff Maxwell Storey had them leave his own coffin in the cell with him the night before they strung him up? Now, what the hell are you gonna say?'

The man mumbled, 'Hang 'em.'

'Let 'em dance,' bellowed McMurtry. 'Weevil, you want to see them dance for you?'

The half-wit, smitten by the excitement, hopped out and began throwing his legs about in a little jig in front of the Rangers. "Oh, you New York gals, can't you dance the polka'!' He danced along before the Rangers until

179

he bumped into Day, then he scurried back behind McMurtry.

'That's the vote and there's no arguin' it,' McMurtry told Day. 'Come on! Let's find a hangin' tree.'

The half-breed jabbed him and Tillet began to move. Except, it seemed that the faces were floating by him. In the gloom of the church there seemed to be nothing visible but pale, shocked faces above white shirt-fronts and blouses. Karl had half risen, staring at them as if he saw something astounding. Anna's lips were twisted apart. Her eyes were fixed on his, but they were glazed, like a blind person's. The next face he saw was Day's. It was white too. His eyes stared hard into Tillet's and then his face, too, floated past.

At the door of the church he stumbled into Nolan. Nolan turned slowly around. His lips were clamped into a white line and his nostrils were flared. His eyes passed over Tillet without seeming to see him.

He heard a hissing whisper from

Cannibal Beal, 'What do we do, Nate? Give us the word. I'm ready.'

Outside the church, the dark sky pressed down low. The trill of a lone bird cut through the still air, loud and shrill. Tillet was light-headed. His body felt hollow and weightless.

A hundred yards from the townside of the church, the oak stood with its thick boughs stretched out. McMurtry's voice rumbled and one of the brothers jabbered something at Nate Sommers. But the words didn't make any sense in Tillet's mind. He was finding it difficult to walk straight.

It came to him that he was dreaming. The thought relieved him so much that he hardly noticed the things that happened next. But at the touch of the rope, he began to doubt. The doubt became a certainty and with a surge of terror he felt the flanks of the horse slip away from between his legs. His body swung back and pulled on his neck with the weight of a mountain. He swung forward and his tongue began to be pushed out of his mouth and his eyes began to swell and bulge out of the eye-sockets. The earth and everything in Creation were just massive weights. They said your body shamed you at the end —

He felt a touch on his arm and almost shouted out. Relief flooded him again: it was a dream after all, and he was coming out of it.

Then he realized that they were tying his hands behind his back.

'Keep off your stinkin' paws!' Cannibal Beal was waving a fist at the little man, who kept his distance, his mouth hanging open, a noose in his hands.

McMurtry stuck out his pistol. 'Get your hands behind your back.'

'Or what? You gonna shoot me? Go ahead.'

'I'll shoot your arms off for you, and you'll hang just the same.' McMurtry aimed the gun at Cannibal's elbow.

The Ranger's fat cheeks were quivering and he looked reckless enough to rush McMurtry. But finally he shoved his hands back to be tied. He dropped his voice low. 'You ain't as stupid as you look, hoss.' The fat on his face was quivering. His lip was pulled back off his teeth. 'You couldn't hardly be.'

McMurtry took the looped lasso off his shoulder and began knotting it. 'Proper hangman's noose has got thirteen turns to the knot. Maybe that's why thirteen is reckoned unlucky.'

'Hurry the hell up!' Day shouted. He spun round and began to pace with jerky strides.

McMurtry finished tying the rope and, dipping his shoulder, he lobbed the noose over a branch.

'Always gotta be some bold gent to lead off the waltz. Which one of you boys it gonna be?'

The long-haired man spoke up. 'We're gonna need four ropes.'

'I figure the others can watch and wait their turn,' said McMurtry.

'Ain't no call for . . . ' The long-haired man shook his head and let his words trail away.

Day Hanly snatched a lariat from out of the half-breed Ramon's hands and came striding across. 'You're a sorry bastard, McMurtry.' He threw the rope over a branch. 'Get your rope over here, Torrence.' The long-haired one and the one with the broken nose followed Hanly's example.

The two half-breeds laid hands on Beal, but the Ranger snarled and shook them off, and walked over to one of the nooses and let them put it over his head. Before they could be touched, Sommers and Nolan walked over to the tree. Tillet watched them as the nooses were dropped over their heads. Nolan was rigid. Nate Sommers was looking off into the distance with a frown of concentration on his face, but he came back from wherever he was when Nolan spoke his name. Nolan looked into his eyes and seemed to lose whatever it was he was going to say. He sniffed in a breath, faced forward and shifted his feet to steady himself.

Tillet watched this, but it seemed

to be happening far away. The blood was singing in his ears and muffled all the sounds. A sickly, weak feeling was passing through him, dimming his vision. A voice rumbled in his ear. A hand touched him, but he felt it only faintly, as if his arm was covered in wadding. Another hand gripped his arm and Tillet's knees began to give. He sank to the ground.

A voice high up above him came faintly through the blood singing in his ears. 'We're gonna have to carry this one.'

Tillet muttered, 'No . . . '

Somebody laughed up above him. He felt his arm being hauled and heard McMurtry's voice close to his ear. 'Come on, sonny, don't say we got to carry you.'

'Please . . . '

'What?' He could feel McMurtry's breath on his face as he stooped close to hear.

'Please . . . '

McMurtry laughed. 'I'll be — he's

beggin'. He's sayin' please.'

Hanly screamed, 'McMurtry, you puke-lickin' dog . . . leave him be, or I swear I'll put a bullet in your rotten heart.'

Tillet felt the hands release him. He put a hand to his forehead and found it was icy cold.

'Now, we out-voted you on this, Day.' McMurtry was trying for a reasoning tone. But there was wariness in it. 'They all got to hang. We decided on that.'

'You want to shoot with me, McMurtry?' McMurtry didn't reply. There was no mistaking that Day was on the point of action, coiled up for it like an animal about to spring.

On his knees, Tillet twisted round and put his hands on the ground.

'Any of you want to throw down on me?'

He looked up over the grass and saw the farmers watching intently, like an audience, bunched at the door of the church. He could see how Anna's eyes glittered, but seemed glazed and as unseeing as a blind person's. The light-headed, sick feeling swept over him again and he bent over to let the blood to his head.

'Torrence? Paco? And what about you, Bill?'

Tillet turned away from the eyes of the farmers.

They were all looking at Day, scared. He was sending off waves of danger, like a snake about to strike.

'I know what you feeling, Day,' Paco said. 'He was your partner once. But I think you a better frien' to him than he ever was to you.'

'It don't matter about that. I don't style myself the voice of justice, like McMurtry. When a man asks me for mercy, I'm gonna give it.' Hanly stood and eyed them. The muscles of his jaws stood out in hard ridges. They avoided his glance, fearing the recklessness they could see in his eye.

The silence was broken by a little snort of laughter from McMurtry. 'Hell, let him go then. If he ain't got the balls to die game, he ain't even worth hangin'.'

Hanly sprang. Three running strides took him to McMurtry and his gun was in his hand before McMurtry could react. He was trying to ram the gun-barrel into McMurtry's forehead, and McMurtry retreated from it running until his back slammed up against the oak.

'Are you game to die?' Hanly cried.

'Day, you're loco.' McMurtry ground his head back against the tree as if he would push it through the bark. His eyelids twitched, his eyes flinching from the sight of the gun-barrel sticking into his face.

'I'm gonna kill you, McMurtry.'

'Day . . .'

'Beg for your life, McMurtry, or I swear I'm gonna murder you.'

'Day . . .' Day's eyes bored into McMurtry's, which dodged and evaded his. 'Come on, men,' he appealed, 'he ain't got the right to do this.'

Pollock spoke. 'You were enjoying yourself a little too much for my liking a minute ago with that there noose. I reckon Day's teaching you a lesson.'

Hanly cocked the .45's hammer.

The dry, double click made McMurtry screw shut his eyes. 'Day, for the love of . . . ' At the word 'God' his throat began trying to swallow at the same time. His head began twitching so that his hat, caught against the bowl of the tree, began to bob up and down.

'Not good enough, McMurtry.'

McMurtry found his voice and got out the word, 'Please.'

'Ah, hell, I reckon I'll just kill you anyhow.'

'Oh, Jesus Lord, don't shoot.' McMurtry began clutching at the lapels of his own coat. His eyelids closed tight, he began with his left hand to pat gingerly at the barrel of the gun, touching it as if the steel was hot, trying to push it away, until Hanly rapped him on the fingers with it. 'Oh, dear God,

I'm begging you — Day, don't shoot me.'

Hanly lowered the gun from McMurtry's forehead and eased down the hammer.

'See? Not so easy to be game when your last chance is gone. When you're looking at certain death and there ain't no choice but kiss the world goodbye . . . ain't so easy to keep cheerful then, is it?'

He called over to Tillet. 'Get up, Johnny.'

Tillet felt he should stay on his knees. He wanted to find a dark hole and burrow into it. But he got to his feet and stood lifelessly, drained of will.

Day, the sense of his power flowing back into him, stood easily in front of the Rangers. 'Day Hanly ain't never killed a man who hadn't got a weapon in his fist.'

He walked up close to Nolan. 'You're a blade for the ladies, I reckon. Me and you could've been friends. I can tell it.

Except you keep the way of the law and I run the outlaw's path. Just imagine, though, if the tables were turned — if you'd brought me in, and I was facing a rope. I guess I could plead till the cows come back to some hatchet-faced old judge, and it wouldn't do me a bit of good. That's the law — cold as the brass handle to a coffin. But now you, you just ask the once and Day Hanly, fearsome outlaw as he is, will let you go free.'

The Ranger's eyes were wide and staring. They rolled to the side as if looking for a prompt from the other two.

'It ain't no shame. When every last chance is gone . . . ' Day turned to Cannibal Beal. 'Come on, give him the lead, big man. Just ask me please and I'll let you go.'

Beal turned his one eye on him. There was a hard flat certainty in it. He said, 'You're talkin' to a Texas Ranger, mister.'

Hanly's jaw muscles clenched. He

stared hard at Beal and for a second it looked like he might strike him. He turned back to Nolan. 'You've got all your life ahead of you. Say that one little word and I'll let you walk.'

Nolan frowned suddenly and blurted out, 'By God I won't.'

Hanly's eyes filled with fury. He spun away from Nolan, strode up to Sommers and shouted, 'Well?'

Nate Sommers did not look at him. He kept his eyes fixed on the distance and said quietly, 'Get away from me.'

Hanly stood with his face inches from Sommers'. He was quivering, his face dark with blood. Fury seemed to build in him like pressure in a piston, making his eyes bulge from their sockets. Suddenly he yelled, and spittle flew into Sommers' face. 'Well, hang then and be damned.'

He ran over and caught hold of Cannibal's rope. 'Give me a hand.' Torrence and one of the half-breeds came running up and the three of them hauled back on the rope until the Ranger rose kicking into the air. Hanly left the two of them to hold the weight and took the slack round the trunk of the tree and made a hitch. The two let go the rope and Beal dropped. The hitch caught and he jerked and bounced back up on the swing of the branch.

'Move it.' Hanly's voice sounded on the edge of control but it acted like a whiplash on the other two. They ran for Nolan's rope, heaved until he rose two feet in the air. They hitched him and without slacking pace ran for Nate Sommers' rope and hauled until his toes left the ground.

The three figures dangled, turned slowly in different directions on the ropes. Nolan was kicking furiously. Tillet heard a rising mutter and a shrill female cry of horror. The farmers began to surge forward. But the half-breed called Ramon, growling like a dog, made a run towards them waving his gun threateningly and the farmers halted. Dolores, engulfed by the farmers' advance, ran out from among them and over to Day.

Day put his arm around her and began to hurry her away into the town. 'Come on out of here.'

As the others began to follow, McMurtry protested, 'If we leave them, the nesters'll cut them down.'

Without looking back, Day yelled, 'I don't care.'

A blast seemed to slap the low sky and echo back down. Day's hat was whipped off his head.

Day spun round, both guns in his hands. Dolores had begun to run away from him, but another blast made her waver, her hands flapping at the sides of her face, then dash back to clutch on to the back of Day's shirt as he began blazing with both guns.

Tillet saw McMurtry pitch over on to his face as he sprinted for the shelter of the tree on which the Rangers dangled. Day holstered a gun and, firing with the other, dragged Dolores to the cover of the tree, where he pushed her down into the hollow of a root, flattened his back against the trunk and began reloading.

One of the half-breeds and Pollock had scrambled behind the bole of another, smaller oak. Torrence and the other half-breed had fallen prone on the ground and were shooting into the scrub behind the church.

'Stop! Hang fire!' Day shouted.

'Where the hell are we firing at?' screamed Torrence in the echoing silence that fell when the guns ceased.

'Over at the corner of the church. Anybody see who it was?'

Dolores, crouched down under the big curving root, began to wail, 'Oh. *Dios*. It is me he wants to kill.'

'Who?'

For answer, Dolores let out another terrified wail.

'You know I'll have to die before anyone touches you,' Day told her.

The blast of the heavy-calibre rifle slapped the air. An explosion of gunfire answered it. Through the gunsmoke, Tillet saw Day race out from the cover of the tree. The half-wit dashed after him. The sound of Dolores screaming Day's name came faintly through the roar of guns. Pollock jumped to his feet and began to run after Day. The half-breed tried to grab him, screamed something in Spanish, and shot him. Pollock's legs gave as if he'd been slammed behind the knees.

Half-a-dozen horses were tethered outside an abandoned rooming-house at the edge of town. They were dancing and snorting and the one that Day loosed began running even before he was in the saddle. Day wrenched it viciously around. It stumbled, went down on one knee, then was up and galloping back into the shooting. Day rode straight for the corner of the church. At the last minute, he dropped the reins, drew both guns and began blazing.

Simultaneously, Day disappeared behind the church and a small figure, holding a rifle as big as itself, staggered into view.

Tiller could see two red stains spreading on the boy's yellow cotton shirt.

'Heinz!' Gunter Stitt broke from the group of farmers and started towards the boy.

The boy had his eyes squeezed closed. He let fall the rifle and threw out his arms at the sound of his name, but turned in the wrong direction. Gunter, crouching forward as if he'd been kicked in the belly, his right hand reaching out, came up behind the boy. At the touch of his father's hand on his shoulder, the boy gave a little gasp and dropped like a stone. Tillet was sure he was dead.

Day Hanly had made a circuit of the church and came riding back up. He reined, and gazed down at the boy. There was a wild and stricken expression in his eyes. Gunter lunged for him and grabbed his leg. Day kicked himself free, pulled the horse around and gouged his spurs into its flanks.

Gunter's square, flat-featured face became blank and icy. He stooped down and picked up the rifle.

Dolores had reached the horses and was trying to pull herself on to the back of one. The half-wit was already mounted. When the shooting started again, Day did not look round. Pollock, shot in the leg, trying to hobble towards the horses, threw out his arms and cried for help. Day stopped and hauled him up behind.

Torrence, lying on his back reloading, dropped his gun and clutched his collar-bone. Gunter coolly drew a bead on one of the half-breeds. The rifle jerked to the left as a bullet slammed into his shoulder. But Gunter took aim again, steadying the rifle on his knee. The rifle blasted again and the .50 calibre bullet hit the right side of the half-breed's jaw, flattened, and took away the left side completely. While his brother staggered in a circle, his ragged lower lip flapping away from his gums, the second half-breed jumped out from behind the oak on which the Rangers hung. With a deep-throated bellow he charged towards Gunter, cocking and firing as he ran. A big rifle bullet smashed through his body, lifting a chunk out of his back. It almost carried him off his feet. He staggered sideways like a crab, but regained his balance and kept coming. A burst of sparks flew from the barrel of the Winchester and Gunter's head snapped back. But he ejected a shell and took aim again. Blood was running over his right hand and the stock of the rifle. He squeezed the trigger and the hammer fell on an empty chamber.

The half-breed gave a surprised shout of laughter and shot Gunter in the head.

He looked down and put a shaking hand to his bloody shirt. A weak groan escaped him, then his lips drew back savagely. 'You child of a whore. You have finished Paco.' He tried to shoot

Gunter again, but his own pistol was empty. He flung it at the farmers, hitting Karl's wife on her shoulder, then he slammed down full-length on to his face.

At this, the farmers unfroze. They began running for the tree on which the Rangers hung.

With difficulty, because of his hands tied behind his back, Tillet raised himself off the ground, where he'd thrown himself when the shooting started. He struggled as far as his knees, but when he tried to lurch from there on to his feet, he overbalanced and went down again. It seemed that his will deserted him then. He knelt, staring at his knees, until he felt someone using a knife on the rope that tied his hands.

The priest's voice spoke close to his ear. 'Two are still alive. The one they call Cannibal is dead.'

He glimpsed other feet approaching. Pushing himself up quickly, he retreated from them. The priest called his name.

He kept his head low and mumbled something in reply. The side gable of the church screened him from their eyes. He made his way into the scrub at the back of the church and then his strength and will deserted him again. He felt weary to death and sat down among the bushes and weeds.

15

A cold rain began to fall and Tillet went into the church. He sat there while the dusk deepened. Thoughts were massing in his head, but they left him alone for now. Somehow he could foretell they would have plenty of time to work on him once they were ready. He sat and watched the dark shapes grow dimmer and disappear until only the pale squares of the windows were visible. The pitch-darkness was a comfort and the feebleness and lethargy he felt was in some way pleasant if only he could sit here without the world bothering him. He remembered he was in a church and half ironically and half seriously he began to pray. 'If You're in the business of helping folk out, I guess I could use a little. They say You favour the meek. I don't reckon You'll get much meeker than me. So where do

I go from here?' After a while he said, 'What's the matter, ain't got no time for cowards? They say St Peter was a coward . . . Well, then, damn You for bringing me to this pass.'

The church door opened. Tillet felt a superstitious fear seize him. For a moment he wondered if an angel had been sent to help him or if he had called a devil with his blasphemy.

A match struck and giant shadows of the pews and pulpit danced on the board walls. Footsteps walked down the aisle. It was only the priest. He carried the lantern to the end of the aisle before he turned and saw Tillet. He started.

'Name of God! You gave me — ' He came down to where Tillet sat in the pew. 'Though, I thought you'd be here — when I saw your horse tied outside — still, to see you sitting there, calm as you please . . .'

'It must look kinda odd. I been meaning to go . . . 'cept' I feel so tired.'

'Well, let's go back now. Have a bite to eat.'

Tillet felt the priest was talking to him like a grown-up trying to reassure a child. He felt weary again all of a sudden and turned his head away.

The priest sat down and said in a quiet voice, 'What about Anna? It's a fine girl, that, a fine girl.'

'I can't look her in the eye again.'

'You're underestimating that girl. You know, a woman understands a man. His strengths and weaknesses . . . It was only your nerve that failed you. That can happen to anyone, you know.'

Tillet sat silent, resentful of the priest's interfering.

Suddenly, the priest clutched his sleeve and went down on his knees. 'Listen, John, kneel down with me and pray.'

Tillet laughed. He pulled his arm free and stood up. 'I don't belong to your church, Father.'

The priest gazed up with round eyes.

Tillet thought he looked like a pathetic old man.

'Where are you going?'

'I reckon I muddied the waters here for myself. I best start fresh someplace else.'

After he'd untied his horse and mounted, he passed the priest standing at the church holding the lantern above his head. Tillet did not look at him or say goodbye. He felt a sense of freedom and, for a moment, it seemed that the future was full of possibilities. But as soon as he had quit the priest, his spirits slumped again and now he felt like a mangy hound, sneaking through the shadows of the town.

Rain began to spit in his face. He shivered inside his thin shirt. Up ahead, the only light in town was from the windows of Caldwell's saloon. Beyond that nothing could be seen but the outline of the pine-topped hills against a pale band of clear night sky. From the saloon, the smell of alcohol came to him on the clear, chilly air.

The door of the saloon clattered open and a shrill female voice shouted, 'To hell with you. To hell with all of ya. I should never have left New Orleans. Cowboys! Cows are all they're good for. They ain't fit for the company of women.'

The woman fell silent and stood with her head cocked, listening to Tillet's approach. When he entered the pool of light thrown by Caldwell's window, she called, 'Wait!' With a determined swagger, she came squelching through the thin layer of muck on the street and grabbed his bridle. She was a thin-faced blonde. Her hot, troubled eyes glittered up at him. 'You got a match?' She stuck an inch of cigarette with a blackened end into her mouth.

'I'm sorry, I ain't got one, ma'am.' Tillet was surprised at how feeble his voice sounded, but it seemed to make a favourable impression on the woman. Her thin lips curved open in a smile. 'You're just a kid, ain't you? Where was you going?' She jerked her thumb over her shoulder. 'This pig-pen is the only place open in town.' He felt her hand like a claw on his thigh. 'You want to *faire amour*?'

'Beg pardon?'

'You can spend the night with me for five dollars.'

'I reckon I'll be spending the night in the saddle. Ain't got no five dollars.' Tillet found his voice was a little unsteady. He tried to keep his leg from jittering under her hand.

'Come on, you can buy me a drink, can't you? What's the matter — afraid to spend your money?'

She tugged on the bridle and the horse followed her obediently to the rail outside the saloon. 'Jump down, cowboy. A dog shouldn't be wandering loose on a miserable night like tonight.'

She spoke companionably and Tillet felt a smile pull at his mouth. He did as he was told. All at once the night seemed unbearably cold and lonely and he wanted out of it.

'I ain't welcome in there.'

'You're with me, ain't you? Don't be timid. Look, now, put your arm around me. Put it around me like so. Now, come on.'

There were half-a-dozen people inside the saloon. Over behind the bar, Caldwell glanced up indifferently at Tillet then went back to listening to the doctor, who was talking excitedly, gesturing with his hands. The sheriff sat at a table playing cards with a thin man who worked his fingers nervously at his tobacco-streaked beard. The sheriff looked up and fixed his eye on Tillet with more interest than Caldwell had shown. At a table on the opposite side of the room, the tailor lay slumped over with his head resting on his arms, asleep. The blacksmith sat across from him, his back facing the door.

The blonde stood with Tillet inside the door, her eyes on the blacksmith's back. When he began to turn, she hastily faced front and led Tillet to the bar.

The doctor waggled a finger at Tillet.

'He was there today. At the shoot-out.' He stood examining Tillet with curiosity, wavering a little, breathing heavily through his nose. He dropped a hand on Tillet's shoulder and said, 'I'm gonna buy you a drink. Come on. Glad to see you cut loose from them foreigners. They got queer ways to them. Well, you're with your own now. Luke, give the boy a drink.'

Tillet drank down the whisky poured for him. It glowed in his belly. The blonde's hot body pressed against his side, warming him.

'Tell us all about it — the shoot-out.'

Tillet ran the back of his hand over his tingling mouth. 'I don't want to disoblige you, but I'd like to get my mind off today.'

'Oh, come on.'

'He don't want to talk about it. Leave the kid be.'

'He's gonna have to talk to me about it,' the sheriff said. 'I'll have to make a report out on it.'

'He can do that tomorrow. Let him relax now. Come on, let's you and me sit over here. Buy us a couple of drinks.'

Tillet fumbled the couple of dollars he had earned from the farmers out of his pocket. He paid for the drinks and let the blonde lead him to a table near to where the blacksmith and the tailor sat.

Tillet sipped his drink. The whisky was strong, comforting as a warm hearth-side to a weary traveller. The blacksmith came and leaned on the table. 'Look at her sittin' there.' His manner was bantering and crafty. The way his eyes were hidden behind the narrowed lids added a bashful touch to it. 'Looks like an angel that's just slipped out of Heaven for a shot of rot-gut.'

'I'm a prostitute,' the blonde said defiantly. 'I don't care who knows it.'

'You're a bar-room angel, Flo. And that's as good a trade as mine, according to me.' He held out his hand to Tillet. 'The name's Frank.'

'John.' Tillet shook the blacksmith's hand.

'John, you handsome swine, you stole my girl. But, that's all right; I ain't the jealous type.' He reached in his pocket and dropped some coins on the table. 'To prove I hold no hard feelings — there . . . why don't you go up and get the three of us a drink, John.'

'Tell him to put mine in a fresh glass, John, honey. I hate drinking from a glass with lip-rouge on it — even if it's my own.'

The blacksmith and the blonde kept up a steady banter. Tillet was content to sit quietly sipping his drinks and listen. Once, something that Flo said made him shake with laughter. Each time he stopped, the humour of it would hit him again and the laughter would come bursting out through his teeth. At the end, there were tears pouring out of his eyes.

'That tickled your funny bone,

dearie, didn't it?' Flo's stricken, forty-year-old eyes glittered at him, puzzled but indulgent.

The blacksmith said he had to step over to his shop. 'I'll be back later.' He held out his hand. 'See you, John.'

Tillet knocked a glass over as he stuck out his hand to take the blacksmith's.

A drink or so later, he had an urge to speak his feelings, and he found he was bold enough to do it. 'Flo, you're a fine woman.' His voice was a little slurred. 'I count it a privilege to take a drink with you.'

'I ain't never led a man on, I'll say that for myself. I'm square — even if I am a prostitute.'

'The thing is, we all got our faults. A man's a man for all that, my daddy used to say. Poor Daddy, he weren't much good neither. Couldn't even stand up to my ma. Yeah . . . but it's true what he said — a man's a man for all that.' Bit by bit, things were falling into place in Tillet's mind. Things began to make sense and he could see the truth of them. He wanted to explain and share it with her, but he couldn't find the exact way to say it. He stumbled and got tangled up in his words. He found himself saying, 'You're a beautiful woman, Flo . . . I love you.' He never would have thought to hear himself say these words. It wasn't his way. But now they were coming out easily and naturally. Because he meant them.

The blonde smiled and crinkled up her eyes, gazed happily at him as she blew cigarette smoke in his face.

Sometime later, the doctor came and whispered in her ear and they both disappeared.

Tillet felt happy just to sit and sip his whisky and think things over, now that things made sense. He drained his glass and, pushing himself to his feet, made his way to the bar. When he brought out his money, he found himself holding just a couple of cents in the palm of his hand.

'Looks like you're busted.'

'I reckon.'

'Well . . . I'll tell you what.' Caldwell gave him a wink. 'Seeing as Harvey there's asleep, you can have his job.' Caldwell reached under the bar and came up with a tin pail which he reached over to Tillet. A scum of black dirt coated the inside, and a mess of egg-shells, chicken bones and cigarette butts covered the bottom. 'Take yourself a walk around. Pick up the butts off the floor. When you're done, I'll let you have a shot.'

The sheriff said, 'Come on, I won't bite you,' as Tillet hesitated by his table. Tillet reached under and gathered the butts.

Over at the door as he reached down for a butt, he overbalanced and went over, slowly, but unable to stop himself, until he finished up on his side on the floor.

He felt a hand under his arm. 'Up you come, John.' The blacksmith grinned his narrow-eyed grin. 'Havin' yourself a little roll on the floor, you was, there.'

Flo was back, standing drinking at the bar, when he came to return the pail and claim his drink. She was quiet now, seemed a little sad and truculent. Tillet stood close to her, put his hand on her hip. She did not object but she did not respond either. But after a while, she wrapped her arm in his and said. 'Come on, sweetheart. Mammy's gonna rock you to sleep.'

In the dark corridor that led to the bedrooms, somebody else joined them. He heard the blacksmith's voice, but he couldn't make out what he was saying.

'What about poor John?' Flo said.

He heard coins clinking one on top of the other and the blacksmith's voice saying, 'Every one a silver dollar.'

Flo said to him, 'I'm sorry, sweetie. This is business.'

Tillet felt her arm leave his. Whispering came from further down the corridor. He glimpsed their silhouette against the window at the end. Then he felt her arm wrap around his again. She led him along the corridor and opened a door.

She called, 'Vi'let . . . '

A woman's voice answered from inside the room. The blonde said, 'Will you do me a favour, Vi'let? I picked up a kid. He's got no money and no place to go and I taken pity on him. Will you take him in? I got custom.'

'Yes, I will, Flo dear. I owe you more than that. More'n I can ever repay.'

The door closed behind Tillet and he groped his way into the room. The bed rattled as he stumbled into it.

'Careful, dear.' Her voice was soft, a little feeble, as if she weren't in the best of health.

He couldn't see a thing, except for some objects on the table outlined against the window — a lamp, a jug, some bunched-up garment. The bed was warm. His hand found her, and her body under the cotton nightgown was soft and warm to the touch. As he lay down beside her, the room began to spin. He sat up, but that wasn't any better. There were some matches under his hand on the table. He fumbled for one and struck it on the bed-frame.

'Don't light the lamp, dear.'

'I got to get some light — I — my head — '

The flame of the lamp drove off the whirling darkness and the room came to rest. Tillet turned back to the woman.

A big black insect sat on her forehead, between her eyebrows.

'I got the pox,' she said. She held out her arms. 'Don't be afraid, dear. There's only one way you can get it. I know what to do.' Her arms slid ground his neck and drew him down.

Tillet felt his stomach heave. He didn't have time to put a hand to his mouth or turn away. He belched and the whisky came spurting out.

The woman wailed and Tillet reeled away from the bed. As he staggered, trying to drag on his pants, crashing into the bars of the bed's base and the wall, she howled a stream of sewer filth at him. Something hard struck him on the back of his neck. He jammed his arms into his shirt-sleeves, grabbed up his boots and gunbelt and lurched for the door.

The muffled voice of the blonde came from another room. 'Vi'let? What's the matter? Oh my God, what's he done to you?'

A door opened, throwing another pool of light into the corridor. The blacksmith appeared in the frame. 'What you up to?'

'Get him, Frank.'

As the blacksmith came for him something banged him on the side of the head. The sheriff's voice came through the roaring that filled his ears. 'Making trouble? Come on. We'll see about that.'

He went clattering down the stairs held by a handful of shirt collar, his arms, and the seat of his pants. They rushed him out the door. There were some slaps and punches about the ears, then a boot that landed squarely in the cleft of his buttocks and jarred on the base of his spine stretched him on his face in the muck.

He rode without thinking, taking the same way out as he'd first come into town. The two whores were letting themselves go in a fit of hysterics and their voices followed him like the shrieking of damned souls.

When he reached the parting of the roads, he reined and sat slumped in the saddle. The horse snorted impatiently, but he sat on. He had no heart or will to take one road or the other.

His father had told him how in the old country they'd bury a hanged man at a crossroads then, when the ghost rose, it would not know which path to take. The spell of the crossroads was on him too. It wasn't confusion that paralysed him, just that the thought of going on filled him with a bleak weariness.

'I reckon if I had the guts I'd finish it with a bullet.'

The horse tossed its head as if it sensed his will had deserted him and resented carrying a rider not fit to master it.

'But I ain't. Ain't got the guts.'

The clouds had broken up and the starlight was enough to see by. The soft ground showed hoof-prints going east. The tracks weren't a day old. He guessed they were Day's.

By the side of the crossroads the weathered and split Wells Fargo sign-post stood listing towards the eastward road. The arm pointed down it said the town of Redemption lay in that direction. He had heard it was a ghost town. It had died when the mines played out. Tillet twitched the right rein. The animal jerked the bit back peevishly. Tillet's brow lowered and his teeth clenched. He doubled his fist and punched the horse hard on the ear. When he jabbed with his spurs it obeyed and began to follow the fresh tracks east.

16

There was a glow of light from the saloon, but the windows were too grimed to see through. Tillet peered through a crack between two of the shrunken boards of the door. A candle on the bar shed a dim glow, but the darkness pressed close around it. Day Hanly was kneeling on the ground. When his shadow moved, Tillet could make out the figure of a man stretched out on a pallet. The man groaned and moved feebly and Day put a hand to his forehead and muttered something to him.

Tillet gripped the doorhandle and pushed. The door opened with a grating creak until the rotten top hinge gave and it jammed on the boards.

Day got off his knee. 'Dolores . . . thank the Lord. I thought you'd cut out on me.' He peered into the darkness. Then his hand stole to his gun. 'Who's that?'

Tillet edged round the door. Something scurried out of the way of his feet as he stepped across the dusty boards of the saloon. A look of recognition came into Day's eyes. As he opened his mouth to speak Pollock raised his head off the filthy mattress and called out in a slurred voice, 'Keep 'em off me.' He clutched feebly at Day's leg until Day knelt down beside him again. The rat-tails of long hair stuck to his sweaty face. The lids of his eyes opened a little and he muttered, 'They ate Abilene.'

Day patted his shoulder. 'It's all right, Will. It's all right, old hoss.' The man's head sank back and Day stood up. There was a brooding look on his face. It sat strangely on him.

'Well, Johnny . . . ' Day grinned and a ghost of his old, reckless glint came back. 'It sure is good to see you again. Funny, I was just thinking about me and you and how it wasn't so long ago we was both just a couple of ploughboys . . . until I upped and laid that old spade across my daddy's skull, huh? Yeah, me and you was the best of partners. And I guess if I hadn't been so hot-tempered we'd've been partners yet, hey?'

'I guess.'

'Instead, you went respectable, and me, I ain't turned twenty and look at me — a died-in-the-wool desperado. I'm steeped in blood up to the oxters and bound right for Hell. Why, if things go on this way, I look to be a famous badman some day. Ain't it strange how things turn out?'

'It's strange.'

'Hell, I even got my own personal ghost to ha'nt me.' The brooding look came back into Day's eyes. 'Little tow-headed ghost. Not much of a ghost as ghosts go . . . but all mine.' Day straightened and made an effort to rally himself. 'Yeah, I guess we taken different paths, but they've come to a cross again and I'm glad of it. You find me at a low point, Johnny. Outfit's all shot up . . . Dolores — looks like she run out.' His voice faded away. 'If she'd only stuck . . . I guess that's taken the heart outa me . . . ' Day seemed to forget about Tillet. His eyes gazed, wide-open, without seeing, at the confusion of footprints in the dust. Then a sudden fire shot up in his eyes and they locked on Tillet's. 'But I ain't finished yet. I aim to have some fun before old Nick gets a hold of me. We can build up the outfit again, Johnny. Me and you. We'll do it right this time. Get the right sorts. Square fellows that a man can trust. Why, we'll raise all sorts of hell. We'll live free, Johnny. Call no man boss. I got a saddle-bag stuffed with dollars to start us with, too. It splits three ways now — me, Will here, and little Weevil. You can have the full half of my share. You know the type of me. I don't give a damn for money. If I call a man friend he can have the shirt offa my back and the grub offa my plate. Put out your hand, old friend, and shake on it.'

Day stepped forward and took hold of Tillet's wrist. He froze as he was about to clasp hands and turned Tillet's palm up. 'You hurt yourself, Johnny?'

'It ain't my blood. The half-wit, I killed him ... I come to take you in.'

The fire died in Day's eyes. 'So that's the way of it.'

'I reckon.'

Day dropped Tillet's wrist and nodded wearily. He walked away. Without turning he said, 'I'm telling you to walk out the door, Johnny, because if I turn round and you're still standing there I'm gonna kill you.'

'I ain't running.'

Day let his hands fall to his sides and turned around. With his back to the candles his face was invisible. A lizard darted along the bottom of a beam above his head.

'Johnny — don't do it — I got enough sins on my soul.'

Despair had taken Tillet this far, but now his nerves took over. His flesh shrank at the thought of the bullet. He began to twitch and knew that if he didn't make a move soon he wouldn't be capable of lifting the gun.

With a hand that felt like someone else's he fumbled at the butt. There was a double explosion from Day's guns and then Tillet jerked the trigger and felt the .45 kick in his hand.

He opened his eyes which had closed at the sound of the gunfire. Smoke and dust swirled and the fluttering candle made giant shadows leap on the ceiling. There was a sound of groaning, but as he stepped closer he saw it was coming from the man on the mattress who was trying to rise but could only manage to lift his head. Day was stretched out, a gun still in his right hand. Tillet knelt beside him.

Day spoke in a shaking voice. 'Where am I hit?'

'In the side.'

There was a stain just above Day's left hip. But then he spotted another under his right armpit. Day saw the direction of Tillet's stare.

'It taken itself a journey and reamed me out.'

Blood was eating into the dust around his shoulder and arm.

Day's eyes began to turn up. He blinked hard. 'Dear God, I'm dying. I know it.' He clutched Tillet's arm. He was trembling and his eyes were wide and frightened.

'Johnny, I'm a'scared of going to Hell.'

'The Lord's merciful, Day.'

'Yeah, the Lord's merciful — it's true. He knows I never meant to kill that kid. I ain't evil — in my heart I ain't — just another poorboy gone bad — the Lord knows that. He knows.'

'Best you make your peace, Day.'

Day nodded eagerly. His lips moved rapidly as he whispered his prayer.

Day's mumbling stopped and his lips drew back off his teeth. 'Devil's come for me, Johnny.'

'It's all right, Day.'

Day's eyes were wide with terror.

'Devil's come for my soul.'

'He can't get you. You're in the Lord's — '

Tillet glimpsed something out of the corner of his eye. He rolled his eye back and the hairs stood up on his neck. In the gloom beyond the candlelight he could make out a black shadow with the outline of a man.

The figure approached. The pale face caught the dim glow of the candlelight and the thin Spanish features took shape. Tillet caught the glint of gunmetal.

'Keep away.' Day tried to push himself back.

Tillet gripped his shoulder. 'He's a man like us.'

'Like you?' His lips drew up like a dog's, showing the gums and the top of the teeth. Candlelight flickered rapidly in the black eyes. 'Dirt born of dirt. Fathers — dirt, and mothers dirt. And their fathers and mothers — dirt. They whelped like animals — in some Whitechapel gutter, or Irish hovel, some

228

dismal Norwegian fjord. With peasants like you she betrayed me. *Dios*. Dirt calls to dirt.'

Tillet could see veins and tendons standing up like wires on the hand that held the gun.

'Would you cheat the Devil?'

'Get away from me.'

Tillet felt Day straining and tightened his grip on his shoulder. 'He's only a man.'

'The Devil was the brightest of God's angels. And when he fell . . . there is no middle path for great spirit: that is our tragedy.'

He moved closer and leaned further into the candlelight. Tillet could see dried snot on his moustache and the dirt engrained in the folds of his face. The stink of a goat came from him. 'I have brought her to you.'

'Dolores!'

He swung his right arm from behind his back and the hand held a small travelling grip. The canvas strained at the handles and the bottom was stained dark. 'She is here.' Drops were falling from the sodden canvas. They made a trail of red splashes from Day's chin to his right eye-socket.

Day's right eye was closed. The other bulged wide open. 'Damn your rotten soul.' The gun in his hand roared and smoke billowed against the man's black coat.

He nodded. 'Die with a curse on your lips. Fly straight to Hell.'

There was another explosion and a fan of blood shot out around Day's head. The gun swung towards Tillet. 'Did you also have the *puta*?'

His chest heaved and he coughed a gout of blood on to his beard. He collapsed across Day, and the bag in his hand was jammed between them both. His face was in Day's brains. His eye rolled back and locked on Tillet's, but apart from that he did not move.

17

Billows of white cloud rose high into the vast blue Texas sky. The autumn morning was warm but the birds could sense the winter blizzards ahead and were winging south.

Nate Sommers took a quid of chewing tobacco from his pocket. He looked around the neat porch, with its vine-trellises and baskets of dried wild-flowers, where the farmers sat with grave faces staring at their hands, and thought better of it.

The women had washed and prepared the bodies of Gunter, Heinz and the Ranger. Now they were making a meal for the men.

As he put the quid back in his pocket, he noticed riders against the skyline. There were two of them, leading three horses.

Mrs Miller came out and spoke in

German. Then, for the benefit of the two Rangers and the priest, she said, 'Please, the food — it is ready.'

Now some of the others had spotted the newcomers. As they drew nearer, it could be seen that one of them was Tillet. Soon they could see that the three horses he led had bodies stretched across their backs. The man with the long hair beside Tillet swayed in his saddle as he rode.

The priest stood up. His brows were drawn down in a frown and he stared hard at the approaching riders. 'Praise be His name. The boy was lost, but the Lord found him again and showed him his path.'

The priest gave a quick, up-and-down jerk of his head, set his jaws firmly and hurried down the porch steps.

As Tillet brought the horses to a stop, the man with the long hair sagged and began to fall out of the saddle. Karl sprang to catch him and he and Wolf and Nate Sommers lowered him to the ground.

'He's hurt pretty bad,' Tillet said.

Nate Sommers straightened up. 'He'll live to hang.' His voice was a weak croak. 'You do all this?'

Willie Haufe broke through the rest of the men. He lifted Day's head by the hair and spat in his face.

'Who's this?' Nate Sommers was looking at the corpse on the white horse.

'I don't know him. He had a vendetta against Day. Because Dolores used to be his woman, I guess.'

'What happened to Dolores?' the priest asked.

'She's dead too. I buried her outside of Redemption.' Tillet nodded at the corpse of the thin man. 'He butchered her up. She wasn't fit to see.'

'Poor child.' The priest bowed his head. 'God have mercy on her soul.'

'Well . . . you have picked the right man when you made John a Ranger,' Karl said to Nate Sommers.

Nate Sommers looked at the bodies

and nodded. 'You did good, son. If you want to stay with the company permanent, you'll have my recommendation.'

Tillet shook his head. 'I reckon the Lord intended for me to shove a plough.'

'In that case,' — Nate Sommers grimaced and fingered his swollen throat — 'you'll be able to buy yourself a handy piece of dirt with the reward on Hanly.'

Tillet got off his horse and made for the rain-water barrel at the side of the house. His legs felt like rubber and he realized how tired he was. Wolf got there before him, pulled off the cover and dipped water with the tin bucket. He held the bucket out. 'Drink, John.'

As Tillet raised the bucket to his mouth, Anna came to the door of the house. Stepping from the darkness of the doorway into the glare of sunshine, she seemed to Tillet's fatigued brain to appear out of thin air, and he held the bucket halfway to his lips and stared at her. Anna, her face screwed up against the bright sunlight, stared back. When Wolf looked round to follow his gaze, Anna turned her head quickly and called something to the farmers. She spoke in her own tongue, but he thought he could hear a shake in her voice.

Karl said, 'We come, my dear. We come.'

Tillet walked back to his horse. The priest watched him take the rein and said, 'As you said yourself, the clay's in your blood. And where better to buy a nice bit of land than right here, where you're among friends? Eh?'

'I see the birds flying south all morning. I taken a notion to follow them.'

'No, my friend.' Karl gripped his arm. 'We do not let you go so easily as you think.'

Another work-roughened farmer's hand imprisoned his other hand. 'No, you must stay now with us.'

'Yes, it is here that he belongs.'

Tillet found himself mounting the porch steps. Half way between waking and sleeping, he might have been floating up them. From the dark opening of the doorway he could hear the soft voices of women and the peaceful chink of plates. At the threshold, an urge to run came to his dazed brain, but the farmers' bodies pressed close and their honest hands held him.

THE END

RIDERS OF RIFLE RANGE
Wade Hamilton

Veterinarian Jeff Jones did not like open warfare — but it was there on Scrub Pine grass. When he diagnosed a sick bull on the Endicott ranch as having the contagious blackleg disease, he got involved in the warfare — whether he liked it or not!

BEAR PAW
Nevada Carter

Austin Dailey traded two cows to a pair of Indians for a bay horse, which subsequently disappeared. Tracks led to a secret hideout of fugitive Indians — and cattle thieves. Indians and stockmen co-operated against the rustlers. But it was Pale Woman who acted as interpreter between her people and the rangemen.

THE WEST WITCH
Lance Howard

Detective Quinton Hilcrest journeys west, seeking the Black Hood Bandits' lost fortune. Within hours of arriving in Hags Bend, he is fighting for his life, ensnared with a beautiful outcast the town claims is a witch! Can he save the young woman from the angry mob?

GUNS OF THE PONY EXPRESS
T. M. Dolan

Rich Zennor joined the Pony Express venture at the start, as second-in-command to tough Denning Hartman. But Zennor had the problems of Hartman believing that they had crossed trails in the past, and the fact that he was strongly attached to Hartman's Indian girl, Conchita.

BLACK JO OF THE PECOS
Jeff Blaine

Nobody knew where Black Josephine Callard came from or whither she returned. Deputy U.S. Marshal Frank Haggard would have to exercise all his cunning and ability to stay alive before he could defeat her highly successful gang and solve the mystery.

RIDE FOR YOUR LIFE
Johnny Mack Bride

They rode west, hoping for a new start. Then they met another broken-down casualty of war, and he had a plan that might deliver them from despair. But the only men who would attempt it would be the truly brave — or the desperate. They were both.

THE NIGHTHAWK
Charles Burnham

While John Baxter sat looking at the ruin that arsonists had made of his log house, a stranger rode into the yard. Baxter and Walt Showalter partnered up and re-built the house. But when it was dynamited, they struck back — and all hell broke loose.

MAVERICK PREACHER
M. Duggan

Clay Purnell was hopeful that his posting to Capra would be peaceable enough. However, on his very first day in town he rode into trouble. Although loath to use his .45, Clay found he had little choice — and his likeness to a notorious bank robber didn't help either!

SIXGUN SHOWDOWN
Art Flynn

After years as a lawman elsewhere, Dan Herrick returned to his old Arizona stamping ground to find that nesters were being driven from their homesteads by ruthless ranchers. Before putting away his gun once and for all, Dan forced a bloody and decisive showdown.

RIDE LIKE THE DEVIL!
Sam Gort

Ben Trunch arrived back on the Big T only to find that land-grabbing was in progress. He confronted Luke Fletcher, saloon-keeper and town boss, with what was happening, and was immediately forced to ride for his life. But he got the chance to put it all right in the end.

SLOW WOLF AND DAN FOX:
Larry & Stretch
Marshall Grover

The deck was stacked against an innocent man. Larry Valentine played detective, and his investigation propelled the Texas Trouble-Shooters into a gun-blazing fight to the finish.

BRANAGAN'S LAW
Alan Irwin

To Angus Flint, the valley was his domain and he didn't want any new settlers. But Texas Ranger Jim Branagan had other ideas. Could he put an end to Flint's tyranny for good?

THE DEVIL RODE A PINTO
Bret Rey

When a settler is cut to ribbons in a frenzied attack, Texas Ranger Sam Buck learns that the killer is Rufus Berry, known as The Devil. Sam stiffens his resolve to kill or capture Berry and break up his gang.

THE DEATH MAN
Lee F. Gregson

The hardest of men went in fear of Ford, the bounty hunter, who had earned the name 'The Death Man'. Yet even Ford was not infallible — when he killed the wrong man, he found that he was being sought himself by the feared Frank Ambler.

LEAD LANGUAGE
Gene Tuttle

After Blaze Colton and Ricky Rawlings have delivered a train load of cows from Arizona to San Francisco, they become involved in a load of trouble and find themselves on the run!

A DOLLAR FROM THE STAGE
Bill Morrison

Young saddle-tramp Len Finch stumbled into a web of murder, lawlessness, intrigue and evil ambition. In the end, he put his life on the line for the folks that he cared about.

BRAND 2: HARDCASE
Neil Hunter

When Ben Wyatt and his gang hold up the bank in Adobe, Wyatt is captured. Judge Rice asks Jason Brand, an ex-U.S. Marshal, to take up the silver star. Wyatt is in the cells, his men close by, and Brand is the only man to get Adobe out of real trouble . . .

THE GUNMAN AND THE ACTRESS
Chap O'Keefe

To be paid a heap of money just for protecting a fancy French actress and her troupe of players didn't seem that difficult — but Joshua Dillard hadn't banked on the charms of the actress, and the fact that someone didn't want him even to reach the town . . .

HE RODE WITH QUANTRILL
Terry Murphy

Following the break-up of Quantrill's Raiders, both Jesse James and Mel Becher head their own gang. A decade later, their paths cross again when, unknowingly, they plan to rob the same bank — leading to a violent confrontation between Becher and James.

THE CLOVERLEAF CATTLE COMPANY
Lauran Paine

Bessie Thomas believed in miracles, and her husband, Jawn Henry, did not. But after finding a murdered settler and his woman, and running down the renegades responsible, Jawn Henry would have time to reflect. He and Bessie had never had children. Miracles evidently did happen.

COOGAN'S QUEST
J. P. Weston

Coogan came down from Wyoming on the trail of a man he had vowed to kill — Red Sheene, known as The Butcher. It was the kidnap of Marian De Quincey that gave Coogan his chance — but he was to need help from an unexpected quarter to avoid losing his own life.

DEATH COMES TO
ROCK SPRINGS
Steven Gray

Jarrod Kilkline is in trouble with the army, the law, and a bounty hunter. Fleeing from capture, he rescues Brian Tyler, who has been left for dead by the three Jackson brothers. But when the Jacksons reappear on the scene, will Jarrod side with them or with the law in the final showdown?

GHOST TOWN
J. D. Kincaid

A snowstorm drove a motley collection of individuals to seek shelter in the ghost town of Silver Seam. When violence erupted, Kentuckian gunfighter Jack Stone needed all his deadly skills to secure his and an Indian girl's survival.

INCIDENT AT LAUGHING WATER CREEK
Harry Jay Thorn

All Kate Decker wants is to run her cattle along Laughing Water Creek. But Leland MacShane and Dave Winters want the whole valley to themselves, and they've hired an army of gunhawks to back their play. Then Frank Corcoran rides right into the middle of it . . .

THE BLUE-BELLY SERGEANT
Elliot Conway

After his discharge from the Union army, veteran Sergeant Harvey Kane hoped to settle down to a peaceful life. But when he took sides with a Texas cattle outfit in their fight against redlegs and reb-haters, he found that his killing days were far from over.

BLACK CANYON
Frank Scarman

All those who had robbed the train between Warbeck and Gaspard were now dead, including Jack Chandler, believed to be the only one who had known where the money was hidden. But someone else did know, and now, years later, waited for the chance to lift it . . .

LOWRY'S REVENGE
Ron Watkins

Frank Lowry's chances of avenging the murder of his wife by Sol Wesley are slim indeed. Frank has never fired a Colt revolver in anger, and he is up against the powerful Wesley family . . .

THE BLACK MARSHAL
John Dyson

Six-guns blazing, The Black Marshal rides into the Indian Nations intent upon imposing some law and order after his own family has been killed by desperadoes. Who can he trust? Only Judge Colt can decide.

KILLER'S HARVEST
Vic J. Hanson

A money man and a law deputy were murdered and a girl taken hostage by four badmen who went on the run. But they failed to reckon on veteran gunfighter Jay Lessiter, or on Goldie Santono's bandidos.